ANGEL BABY

ALSO AVAILABLE BY BRENDA LYNE

NOVELS

Charlie's Mirror

Sister Lost

The Thirteenth Cabin: A Raegan O'Rourke Mystery

SHORT STORY COLLECTIONS

Bourbon & Burlap

ANGEL BABY

A Raegan O'Rourke Mystery

BRENDA LYNE

Brenda
Lyne
Books

Copyright ©2023 by Jennifer DeVries
Writing as Brenda Lyne

Cover design by Susan@yuneepix.com
Book design by Jennifer DeVries

Published in the United States by Brenda Lyne Books

Printed in the United States

ISBN: 978-1-7376133-7-4

First edition: September 2023

brendalyne.com

For my Uncle Al. Thank you for teaching me everything I know about growing tomatoes. Rest in peace.

PART 1:
JESSE

Sunday, July 11, 2021

CHAPTER 1

This was not how I'd envisioned my very first visit would go.

I had only the vaguest idea of where I was going, and I was driving so fast that I nearly missed my turn. River Street was mostly hidden from busy Bridge Street by a large wooden sign that trumpeted **Welcome to River Junction Minnesota The friendliest city in America!** I yanked the wheel just in time and careened around the corner, then slammed the brakes and crept down the narrow, quiet, and shaded street. Huge old oak trees formed a dense canopy overhead that the sun was powerless to penetrate. The dimness felt sinister to me, like the trees had eyes and were watching me slowly drive by.

Nobody in my family ever came to River Junction. The only reason I was here was because Edison and Morgan Faust had kidnapped my father, and I meant to get him back.

I spied a driveway approach ahead. A rusty old wrought iron gate with a decorative letter A on it stood open, its chains hanging and a broken padlock on the ground. Fear pierced my heart. *They're here,* I thought. I parked my SUV in a patch of grass across the street from the gate; I felt better leaving my car and my purse where someone would find them if I didn't make it out of the mansion. I tugged my thin lambskin gloves tighter on my hands and tucked my car key in the waistband pocket of my capri-length leggings. Then I pulled my father's nine-millimeter Glock from my purse and thought briefly of my grandmother's careworn face.

"Go get them, Rae," she said fiercely as she handed me the loaded weapon. "Bring your dad home safe."

"I will, Mimi."

Heart heavy, I sighed and got out of the car. I walked slowly down the long driveway, gun pointed at the ground. Humidity coated the hot summer air, sending rivulets of sweat down my back. The trees were less dense here, and the sun winked through gaps in the leafy canopy. I was reminded of the northwoods, where I'd just spent the better part of a week. Something in my gut pulled at the thought of Wanderer's Resort on Catclaw Lake. *The Catclaw Kids…such a sad story,* I thought, as if it were some distant memory and I hadn't just been there yesterday. So much had happened in the last twenty-four hours…and trauma had a way of distorting the perception of time.

I glanced to my right and caught a glimpse of a turret clad in gray granite towering above the trees maybe a quarter of a mile away. This was The Fortress, the home of Edison Faust – father to Morgan, grandfather to Nicholas, and card-carrying psychopath.

I rounded a gentle curve and there was the Ainsley Mansion, my maternal family's abandoned homestead, looming large ahead of me. It was an impressive two-story Greek Revival structure clad in buff-colored limestone. It looked like it belonged on a Southern plantation.

The house was nothing but a shell now; all of the windows and doors were long gone, exposing the interior to the elements.

My great-great-grandfather Bernard Ainsley had been forced to uproot his family in the late 1930s and move to Minneapolis in an effort to escape a Montague-and-Capulet style feud with his neighbor Stefan Faust – a feud that was still going strong over eighty years later.

I stopped and listened for any sign of the Fausts and my dad. Hearing nothing, I moved stealthily up the weather-worn front steps toward the gaping hole that used to be the front door. I imagined that once upon a time there had been a heavy solid wood door there, mahogany perhaps, with beautiful stained glass windows set in it. That door would have opened on an expansive foyer with a great big staircase that swept up to the second floor. My great-grandmother Grace Ainsley grew up here, and I could almost hear her little footsteps as she chased her cat Buttons through the house. That was before everything changed for her – and all the Ainsley women who came after her.

I forced myself back to the present with a quick shake of my head and squeezed the grip of the gun. Its solidness was reassuring.

Nothing remained of the interior walls and ceilings but old wood framing and exposed lath. I moved toward the stairs, then stopped when I heard a noise. I listened, and there it was again: a thump, followed by a groan. My heart fell to my feet. I moved quickly on tiptoe down the hallway that led to the rear of the house. The cork soles of my sandals silenced the sound of my footsteps on the warped wood floor.

The sound of voices grew louder as I crept down the hall. At the end, to my left, was a large, high-ceilinged room.

I pressed my body against the wall next to the door and risked a peek.

My dad sat on the filthy floor next to a dusty stone fireplace, his hands bound behind him and blood pouring down the side of his face. His hair, once the same fire-red as mine but now mostly white, was plastered to his head with sweat. He stared defiantly at the two men flanking him. Their backs were to me, but I knew immediately that I was looking at Edison and Morgan Faust. Morgan was in his early sixties like my dad, tall and skinny, with long salt and pepper hair that straggled to his shoulderblades. Edison was nearly as tall and skinny as his son, with wild white hair and a humped back. I fought the urge to burst into the room with gun blazing and forced myself to listen to what Edison was saying to my father.

"Your loyalty to your wife is admirable, Liam. Remarkable." Edison had an old man's voice: reedy and a little unsteady. I'd expected a stronger and more authoritative voice from the man who had terrorized my family and my dreams for my entire life. "But you and I both know that I will have what I want. Spare yourself. Don't stand in my way."

My dad spat on the floor; the spittle came within a cat's whisker of landing on Edison's thick-soled white sneaker. "Fuck you. I'll never tell you where she is."

Edison sighed, put out. "If you insist." He gestured at Morgan, who positioned himself at just the right angle to deliver a hard steel-toed kick to my dad's ribs. The first of many, I had no doubt.

It was time to act. Heart racing, I flipped the safety off, stepped through the door, and pointed the gun directly at Edison's head.

"Don't." I said. My voice echoed in the cavernous room.

Startled, all three men looked in my direction. Edison's eyes widened, then narrowed when he realized who I was. "Ah. Raegan. I didn't realize you'd be joining our little soirée today."

I glanced at my dad, who stared back at me intensely. His pale blue eyes snapped. I gave him a little nod and turned my attention back to Edison. "You're going to want to let him go."

He blinked with feigned surprise. "Oh? And what happens if I don't, silly girl?"

My vision flashed red, and I took a few steps toward him. "You'll be breathing through a brand-new hole in your head."

I saw Morgan move in my peripheral vision and adjusted my stance just enough to show I meant business. "Move again, Morgan, and he dies," I snarled.

Edison gestured, and Morgan stilled. Edison assessed me with surprisingly clear jet black eyes as he considered his options. Time had not been kind to Edison Faust; he was eighty years old now, his hawkish face carved with deep wrinkles and grooves. Hair that had once been jet-black was now white and fine as a gossamer spiderweb. Age spots covered his skinny arms and arthritic hands. His gray polo shirt and jeans hung on his skeletal frame. My family's boogeyman – and grandfather to the love of my life – looked like everyone's grandpa at the grocery store. I didn't know what to think of that.

A quick glance at Morgan Faust confirmed that he was standing by, anxiously watching Edison. A deep, poorly-healed scar ran vertically down the right side of his scruffy face; Edison had done that to his own son in a rage after Morgan failed to deliver my mother years ago. The man was pure evil. My finger itched to pull the trigger and finally free my family from his tyranny.

Before I could, Edison turned and ran like a man twenty years younger, disappearing through a door near the fireplace. Morgan followed without a word.

I'd been prepared for just about anything from Edison — except that. "What the fuck," I shouted, and accidentally jerked the trigger. The gun discharged with a deafening *bang*, and a small hole appeared in the door frame. I ran after them and discovered that the door led to a small portico at the rear of the house; from there Edison and Morgan could easily fade into the wild brush that had taken over the once-lush back lawn.

They were gone.

Frustrated, I went back inside. I crouched next to my dad and laid the gun on the floor. The hot air reeked of spent gunpowder. "Are you okay?" I asked.

"I will be once you untie me," he said. His voice was muffled, like my head had been wrapped in a big pillow. The gunshot had been very loud indeed.

I fished my car key from the waistband of my leggings and used it to cut the plastic cable ties that bound his wrists behind his back, then helped him stand up. He waved his arms and shook his hands to get the blood flowing again, then pulled me in for a big hug.

I wrapped my arms around him. He was warm and solid, and *alive*. The enormity of what had just happened, how close my dad came to being the Fausts' next victim, hit me like a freight train, and I burst into tears.

When I finally calmed down, my dad released me and cradled my face in his hands. "You did good, kid." Up close I could see the source of the blood on his face: a small but deep gash in his forehead, just below his hairline. An ugly black bruise was starting to bloom around it.

"I wanted to kill him," I said.

"I know," he said, releasing me and walking over to the door through which the Fausts had escaped. He leaned out and looked both ways. "We'll get him next time."

I pulled my lambskin gloves off my hands and wiped my wet, snotty face. "Now what?" I asked.

Sirens pierced the air, answering my question for him. "Now we wait," Liam said.

I sighed. "What do we tell them?"

He shrugged. "The truth, I suppose."

I decided to explore the room a bit while we waited. There wasn't much left of it. The walls had once been covered with plaster; that was all gone now, exposing wood lath strips. The fireplace was still intact, although filthy and draped in cobwebs. I imagined that this room had once been a library, or maybe a den. Had Grace sat in this room, reading a book or doing schoolwork in front of a roaring fire?

I slowly circled the perimeter, reading inscriptions kids had written or carved on the weathered lath over the years. Most were just words and numbers, like V + K 4EVER and FOR A GOOD TIME CALL CHRISTINA 427-0096 and BUSTER WAS HERE 7-16-03. One on the slatted wall next to the fireplace, right above where my dad had been sitting, caught my eye because it was bigger, drawn over two wood strips, and also included a little

7

sketch. It was a baby's head crudely drawn in black permanent marker, with the letters MIA scrawled next to it in big letters. *I wonder what MIA means*, I thought. *Missing in action? Or maybe it's a name. A baby's name?* It was so different from the rest of the graffiti on the walls that I figured there must be a story behind it. Quickly, before River Junction's finest arrived, I laid my bare fingertips on the inscribed wood and closed my eyes, curious what I might see.

A barrage of visions popped up behind my eyelids. They were of varying quality, some old and some new, and they all showed variations of the same three basic scenarios: high school kids sharing a beer and/or a joint; a young couple having sex in the corner; and local wildlife, mostly raccoons and squirrels, exploring. There was one vision buried deep under the rest that appeared to show something different. I squinched my eyes and focused tightly on that vision; the rest fluttered away like confetti. It was gray and scratchy, and I could just make out the vague silhouette of someone's face and fingers gripping a fat permanent marker. I couldn't get any clearer than that – but something in the shape of the head suggested it was a man.

Suddenly a deep, booming voice called from the front of the house. "River Junction police. Anyone in here?"

Startled, I dropped my hand and opened my eyes.

"They're here," Liam said.

CHAPTER 2

I stepped away from the wall and joined my dad in the middle of the room. "We're back here," he called.

"Raise your hands," I told him.

"Why?"

"Because they're going to come in here with their guns drawn and we want them to see right away that we're not armed."

Liam grunted and held his hands at shoulder level. I did the same. Within seconds two police officers in black uniforms and heavy equipment-laden belts appeared in the hallway, expertly holding their guns in front of them as they inspected their surroundings for threats. They saw us and moved into the room, training their guns on us. A shiver wracked my spine.

"We received reports of a gunshot in this area. Do you have a firearm?" This was the taller and more fit of the two officers. HENDRICKS was embroidered in white on the front of his shirt. He wore his dark blond hair cropped close to his head. His clear green eyes scanned the room and then landed on me. An unexpected tingle bloomed in my chest. I ignored it.

"Yes, sir," I said. "It's on the floor by the fireplace." Where I'd set it while I freed my dad from his cable tie bindings. *I'm gonna get those bastards*, I thought.

Officer Hendricks kept his gun on us and gestured to the other officer, named CHASE, who walked over to retrieve the Glock. He was shorter and beefier than Hendricks, with slightly longer brown hair and heavy eyebrows. He briefly inspected it and then sniffed it. "Fired recently," he said.

"I can explain," my dad said.

"What's your name, sir?" Hendricks asked from behind his gun.

"My name is Liam O'Rourke, and this is my daughter Raegan. We're actually the victims here."

"I'm going to have Officer Chase pat you down to ensure you have no other weapons, and then we'll talk."

We submitted. Every time Officer Chase's hands touched my bare skin, I saw quick snippets in my head of his life's mundane events: standing at the counter at the local donut shop, holding a bavarian cream bismarck and chatting up the staff; sitting in his underwear at home, watching porn on his laptop; turning hotdogs on a gas grill while holding a beer.

When Chase finished and declared my dad and me weapon-free, the officers finally holstered their guns. I breathed a sigh of relief. Hendricks asked me to accompany him to the other side of the room while Chase stayed with my dad. He stopped near the opposite wall, and as he pulled a small notebook and pen from his shirt pocket, he said, "Ms. O'Rourke, my name is Jesse Hendricks, I'm an officer with the River Junction Police Department."

I fought the urge to make a wiseass remark to dispel tension, and simply nodded instead.

He poised his pen over his notebook. "First I'd like to take your information."

I gave him the spelling of my name, my address, phone number, and birthdate. He wrote it all down dutifully, then caught my eyes and said, "Thank you. Did you fire that nine-millimeter a bit ago?"

"Yes."

"Okay. Tell me what happened."

I took a deep breath, started with the panicked phone call from Mimi only a couple of hours ago, and ended with Edison and Morgan escaping out the back door. Hendricks didn't ask who I was talking about when I said the names Edison and Morgan Faust.

"I fired the gun accidentally," I told him, carefully neglecting to mention that I was about to shoot Edison when he'd turned tail and run. "I was surprised. I didn't expect them to just...just *run* like that."

Hendricks made a few notes in his book. "Why did Morgan abduct your dad, do you think?"

I took a couple seconds to debate how to answer that question before settling on a condensed version of the truth. "The men in the Faust family have been after the women in my mother's family, the Ainsleys, since the 1930s."

Hendricks' eyes widened. "You're an Ainsley?"

He'd surprised me. "I - uh, yeah. I am. How do you know the Ainsleys?"

"I grew up in River Junction," he said. "Everyone here knows who the Ainsleys are. And the Fausts." He held his arms out at his sides. "This was your family's home, wasn't it?"

"My great-great grandfather Bernard Ainsley built it," I confirmed.

"And Edison's grandfather Stefan Faust drove him and his family out," Hendricks said. "Local legend."

Huh. I hadn't realized that anyone in River Junction would remember the Ainsleys or know the story of the decades-long feud between the Ainsleys and the Fausts. It got its start in 1937, after Mimi's mother, Grace Ainsley, decided not to marry Benedict Faust, Edison's father. Grace's first vision was of her betrothed torturing and killing her beloved cat. A related business deal between their fathers failed as a result, depriving Stefan Faust and his family of an expected and badly needed financial windfall. Faust men were experts at holding a grudge, and had been trying to get their revenge on Ainsley women ever since. Mimi told me once that the only reason she and I weren't dead yet was because Edison didn't know where my mother was. I said as much to Hendricks.

He thought for a second, pen between his teeth, and then said, "Is it true what they say about the Ainsleys?"

"What do they say?" I asked, my brow furrowing a bit.

"That Grace Ainsley was struck by lightning when she was a girl and ended up with a psychic ability, and every Ainsley woman born after that has it?"

To hear someone utter my family's deepest secret so casually rocked me to my core. I'd worked so hard my whole life to hide my touch from everyone, and a whole *city* already knew about it? My knees started to shake.

"Ms. O'Rourke? Are you all right?"

"I – ah, yes, I'm – I'm okay," I stammered. "I just…I'm just surprised that anybody knows about that."

"So it's true?" His eyes lit up. "Do you have it?"

I nodded and held up the thin, flesh-colored lambskin gloves I still carried in my left hand after taking them off to wipe my face. "I wear these all the time because when I touch things with my bare skin, I see visions in my head of events that happened to or near them."

"So it is true. I'll be damned," Hendricks said, his voice full of wonder. "How – how do you deal with it? It must be overwhelming."

His tone, so believing, so *understanding*, nearly made me cry again. "It can be. I try to use my touch to help people. Until this morning I was an investigative reporter with the Minneapolis Daily News & Review." That meeting, where I told my editor I was quitting, seemed like a hundred years ago now.

Hendricks' eyebrows went up. "Until this morning?"

"I decided to strike out on my own. I want to use my touch as a private investigator to help solve cold cases." I chuckled humorlessly. "If the Fausts would just back off for a bit, maybe I could do that." Then I surprised myself by saying, "I've also developed a bit of an alcohol problem." *Jesus Christ, O'Rourke - he's a cop, not your damn therapist.* But I couldn't help it; Hendricks had a way about him that invited trust and confidence. It probably made him very good at his job. "It's how I cope with a lot of the things I see, plus the constant fear of a Faust finding my mom and decimating my family. That weighs heavy too." *Not to mention keeping my relationship with Nicholas Faust a secret from my family,* I thought but did not say.

"Where is your mom?" Hendricks asked.

"I don't know. She left us and went into hiding in 1989."

His eyes widened. "You would have been just a kid."

"I was seven."

"Wow." He made a note in his book.

"So what happens now? Did you see what Edison and Morgan did to my dad's face?"

Hendricks nodded. "I did. Officer Chase and I will type up our reports, and our sergeant will decide if further investigation is needed. Then the Greenhaven County attorney will decide whether or not to file charges against Morgan Faust for kidnapping and assault. However, the fact that you had a gun and fired it at Edison and Morgan opens you up to possible assault charges as well."

My stomach dropped to my feet. "That was an accident. Besides, I was defending my father. They could have killed him."

"I get it, but the better course of action would have been to call us rather than try to rescue him on your own."

I stared at Hendricks, unable to form words. It had never occurred to me that I could get in trouble for rescuing my dad from the Fausts.

"The county attorney ultimately makes charging decisions, but I'll make sure my report shows the entirety of the circumstances. And there's one other thing."

I raised my eyebrows.

"If the Fausts are charged – and that's a big if – the chances they'll be convicted are slim. They have a long history of wiggling their way out of criminal charges in Greenhaven County." Hendricks sighed. "Edison Faust has an absolute chokehold on this town. Everyone is afraid of him and his son. So nothing ever sticks. Not even when they beat an elderly couple to within an inch of their lives." His voice was bitter.

"Great," I muttered.

Chase crossed the room and approached Hendricks; they turned away from me and spoke in low voices. I found myself wandering back to the fireplace to take another look at the MIA inscription on the wall. Something about it tugged at my heart.

My dad appeared next to me. "I wonder what it means," he said.

"Me too."

The officers broke up their little conference and made their way back to us.

"Okay, you two are free to go," Hendricks said. His eyes flicked from my face to the MIA inscription on the wall and back to my face again, as if he was making a mental note. He pulled a business card from his shirt pocket, wrote something on it, and handed it to me. "If you think of anything else I should know about this incident, give me a call."

I nodded and took hold of the card. Hendricks held onto it for a second, bright green eyes on mine. My heart skipped a beat.

He knew something about that inscription. And I wanted to know what it was.

CHAPTER 3

"Actually," I said and gestured toward the fireplace. "Officer Hendricks, I have a couple last questions before you go."

He followed me. I pointed at the MIA inscription. "I noticed this earlier and can't stop looking at it. Do you know what it means?"

Sadness clouded Hendricks' eyes. "I believe it's referring to Mia Masterson. A local woman who disappeared back in twenty-ten along with her newborn baby girl."

I blinked. "Oh, my god."

"The baby, Isabel, was only a few days old, which makes it even more tragic. Mia and Isabel have been in RJPD's cold case files almost since the beginning. There just weren't any leads." He touched the inscription, traced the baby's head gently with his fingertips. "I knew Mia in high school."

An idea began to form in my mind. "Maybe I can help."

Hendricks dropped his hand. "You think your touch could help solve this case."

"I actually just got back yesterday from a week at a lake resort up north. The cabin my neighbors were staying in burned down on the Fourth of July, killing their dog, and I went up there to see if I could use my touch to figure out how the fire started." I told him how during the course of my investigation, I'd stumbled across another, deeper mystery: the disappearance of two teenagers from the resort twenty-five years earlier. I told him how I'd worked with Kabetogama County Sheriff Chad Overton and solved both cases.

Hendricks listened closely, concentrating on his shoes and nodding as I spoke. When he didn't say anything right away, I took a deep breath and put my idea out there. "I could do like I did with Kabetogama County and work as sort of a consultant with your PD," I offered. "I'd love to help find Mia and Isabel."

Hendricks was silent for so long that I thought he hadn't heard anything I said.

"Raegan?" My dad called from across the room, where he stood by himself, his hands in the pockets of his shorts. His white t-shirt was covered with streaks of blood from his head wound. Officer Chase had disappeared; he was likely sitting in the air-conditioned police cruiser, waiting for his partner.

I tossed Liam my car key. "I'm parked across the street. I'll be out in a few minutes."

He nodded and left. I returned my attention to Officer Hendricks, who now gazed at me with considerably brighter eyes.

"You know something? I've been a patrol officer with RJPD for fifteen years. I love my job, but I really want to be a detective. I've been studying for the exam. My sergeant is supportive. The problem is that River Junction isn't that big, and there are only two detectives in the Investigations division. No room for me to move in."

"Have you thought about moving to a different department?" I asked.

"I'd rather not. This is my home, you know?"

I understood completely. It was the same reason my family chose to stay in Minnesota, within spitting distance of the man hellbent on killing us all.

"But. I heard yesterday that Chief Briggs is going to request funds for two more patrol officers and one more detective in next year's budget." His eyes actually sparkled. "I've been wracking my brain to come up with a way to improve my chances of getting that detective spot if the money comes through. And I think you just gave it to me."

I grinned. "Solving an eleven-year-old missing persons case would sure help, wouldn't it?" My heart fluttered at the idea of working another cold case. *Finding the Catclaw Kids was only the beginning*, I thought. "Show them what you can do."

"Exactly," he said. "Tell you what. I'll talk to my sergeant and my captain tomorrow and see what they think." He held out his hand. "I don't know what the budget is for outside consultants, but it's worth a shot."

Even for someone like me, who went to great lengths to avoid touching anything with my bare skin, the compulsion to shake someone's hand when it's offered is deeply ingrained. I grasped his hand and *then* realized that mine was still gloveless. A vision bloomed behind my eyes, and Hendricks' face disappeared.

∞

The living room of the small suburban rambler was not that big, but it was stuffed full with oversized floral couches and square end tables cluttered with framed photos. A massive oak entertainment center along one wall held a good-sized tube television set and more framed photos. Heavy mauve drapes obliterated a large picture window, floral artwork hung on the hunter green walls, and the dusty rose carpeting showed fresh vacuum tracks. The glow of a tall floor lamp in one corner fended off the encroaching darkness of a late summer evening.

It wasn't an unpleasant room, it was just...claustrophobic. And very 1990s.

A tall man in a brown county sheriff's deputy uniform stood just inside the front door. He had removed his hat and held it respectfully in front of him, below his waist. His face was somber; he was delivering bad news. A petite woman and a teenage boy with a shock of blond hair huddled together, staring at him in absolute horror. Suddenly the woman's hands flew to her face and covered her mouth and nose. She turned and looked at her son with enormous eyes.

The boy just stood there motionless. Shock drained the blood from his face. Then he turned and disappeared down a hallway. The adults watched him go, uncertainty written all over their faces.

∞

Hendricks released my hand and the vision, faded and scratchy like a videotape played hundreds of times, dissipated. "You all right?" he asked. "You seem a million miles away."

I pulled my gloves back on. "All good. Let me give you my number, call me after you talk to your sergeant." We exchanged phone numbers and finally made our way out of the Ainsley Mansion. I gave Hendricks and Chase a brief wave and walked back down the driveway toward my car and my dad.

CHAPTER 4

The sun had begun its descent below the horizon by the time I finally pulled into the driveway of my dad's south Minneapolis home. All I wanted was to crawl into my childhood bed and sleep.

Mimi rushed out to meet us in the driveway, giving us each a big, frantic hug. "Thank god," she said, over and over. Then: "Come inside, get cleaned up, and then I want to hear every single detail."

I grabbed a bottle of water from the fridge and joined my family in the living room. My dad had finally mopped the blood from his face and changed his blood-stained shirt. The wound on his forehead was raw and ugly. My brother Kieran and his wife Annie, who came to town from Eugene, Oregon for a baby shower and got so much more than they bargained for, watched him anxiously from the loveseat. Every light in the room burned, banishing the shadows of impending darkness.

"Are you all right, Dad?" Kieran asked. Looking at my brother was a bit like looking in a mirror; he had the same flame-red hair and ice-blue eyes as our father and me, but his face had a smattering of freckles that mine did not. At age forty, his hair was showing streaks of white and the smile lines on his face were starting to deepen.

"I took Morgan's steel-toed boot to the noggin. I have a bit of a headache, but I'll be okay." Liam threw me a grateful look. "It was about to get a lot worse, and then your sister showed up and chased them off."

"Edison?" Mimi asked. She compulsively wrung her gloved hands. I felt bad for her; this was her worst nightmare scenario. I laid my own hand on hers to still them.

My dad nodded. "He's after Danielle again."

"What is that old lunatic up to this time?" Mimi muttered.

Her question was meant to be hypothetical, but I knew the answer and I very nearly blurted it out. I even started to open my mouth, then quickly made it look like I was about to take a drink of water. My family could not know that I'd been carrying on a clandestine relationship with Morgan's son Nicholas Faust for the past eleven years. If I told them what I knew, I would have to tell them *how* I knew – and break their hearts. Instead I offered, "Whatever it is, he wants to use Mom's touch to help him."

My mother's touch was different from mine and Mimi's. When my great-grandmother Grace Ainsley was struck by lightning at the age of seventeen, she acquired a combination of psychic abilities: psychometry, the ability to receive information about something by touching it, and retrocognition, the ability to see visions of past events. These abilities, referred to in my family as the "touch," had been passed down to every Ainsley girl born since then.

In 1961, while Mimi was pregnant with my mother, Edison Faust slipped dimethylmercury into the vegetable soup she and her sister Pearl were eating for lunch during a shopping trip in downtown Minneapolis. They immediately realized something was wrong and received medical care right away, saving their lives and my mother's life – but my mother was born a few months later with a touch that allowed her to see *future* events rather than past ones. She was the only Ainsley ever born with precognition, thanks to the mercury.

Edison had inadvertently created a new form of the Ainsley touch, and now he desperately wanted to harness it to help him restore the Faust family to the wealth and prominence it had enjoyed when his grandfather, Stefan Faust, was one of the most successful businessmen in River Junction. And because Faust men placed all blame for their family's downfall and subsequent financial struggles on Ainsley women, it was extra important to Edison that my mom be the one to help him get that wealth and prominence back. There had been numerous attempts over the years to strongarm my mother's whereabouts out of my family. All had failed.

According to Nicholas, whatever Edison was up to now had something to do with online auctions. I didn't know what, exactly, because Nicholas failed to glean that information from his grandfather and pass it on to me as promised. That made it impossible for me to warn my family about the latest danger, and my dad nearly paid the price for it. I was still pissed at Nicholas.

Which reminded me; I hadn't looked at my phone in a while. I took another drink from my water bottle and wondered if there was an apology text from Nicholas waiting for me.

"So what do we do now?" Kieran asked. Annie, doe-like eyes wide, entwined her fingers with his. They'd been married thirteen years and lived in the Pacific Northwest nearly all of that time. I didn't think she'd really experienced a Faust yet.

"You and Annie might want to think about heading home," my dad said. "For your own safety."

Kieran snorted. "And leave you three alone, sitting ducks for Edison Faust? Absolutely not."

My dad glanced at Annie, who shook her head vehemently. He sighed and said, "All right, then." Then he turned to Mimi. "It's been a long time since Edison has been this...bold."

"I know. He hasn't attempted a broad daylight kidnapping in..." Mimi paused. "He usually prefers sneak attacks. He must be desperate."

Sneak attacks. I remembered the crisp fall night in October 2010 when I met Nicholas Faust, who had been sent to track me down at a charity masquerade ball and kill me. I'd sensed him sneaking up behind me with a syringe full of succinylcholine and confronted him. He didn't kill me; instead we ended up spending the evening talking, getting to know each other – and falling in love. For the past eleven years we'd carried on a clandestine relationship, keeping our love a secret from our families as a matter of life or death. He promised me then that he would do everything in his power to protect me and my family from his grandfather. It was a promise he'd faithfully kept...until today.

"Maybe it's time to finally move," Kieran offered. "Come to Eugene. Please."

"We can help you find a place," Annie added. "Our next door neighbor is a real estate agent."

Mimi shook her head. "It doesn't matter where we go. Edison Faust is crazy, he's dangerous, and as long as he's alive nothing will stop him until he gets what he wants."

"That begs the question," Kieran said suddenly. His demeanor had shifted from fear to something more like anger. "Why in the hell do we allow Edison Faust to terrorize us like this? Seriously. I'm tired of this bullshit. We know where he is, let's just go and take the fucker out. Morgan too. And the son, what's-his-name. Go on with our lives."

I dug my fingernails into my palm to stop myself from reacting at the mention of Morgan's son. Everyone else in the room stared at Kieran in stunned silence; the family's peacemaker, the one who rarely raised his voice or had a mean word for anybody, had finally been pushed to his limit.

"I know exactly how you feel," my dad said. "Trust me. I've been doing this for over forty years, and I'd be lying if I said the idea hadn't crossed my mind. But taking the law into your own hands is frowned upon in this country, and I decided it wasn't worth leaving my children without both of their parents."

That gave me an idea. "Mom's been in hiding for thirty-two years, and he hasn't gotten to her yet. Maybe that's what we should do too."

All eyes in the room turned and looked at me with varying degrees of irritation. I held my hands up. "Okay, okay, terrible idea. Here's another one, then: we stay and we fight. Keep on doing what we've been doing. And we look for ways to take the Fausts down – legally."

"And what if Edison gets one of us or Mom before that happens?" Kieran asked stubbornly. My dad's close call had rattled him.

"We've made it this far," my dad said. "No reason we can't keep ourselves alive as long as we stay vigilant." He glanced at Mimi. "You're awfully quiet, Emily."

"I'm feeling a bit like Kieran is, to be honest," she said. "I've been living in survival mode my entire life. I try so hard to be careful, to stay vigilant like you say, and it's still not enough. I'm exhausted." That exhaustion was clear on her worn face. "And I'm angry." She curled her gloved hand into a fist and hit the arm of the couch for emphasis. "How *dare* they snatch my son-in-law from his own driveway?"

I thought briefly of Jesse Hendricks, and a realization dawned on me: I didn't know if Edison Faust had anything to do with Mia Masterson's disappearance, but working with the River Junction Police Department on that case could get me in front of other cases he or Morgan were involved in.

"I say we stick with the status quo, and here's why," I said. I filled them in on what I'd been doing up north all week, investigating a couple of perplexing mysteries, and how I felt like working as a private investigator to help solve cold cases was my true calling. I even had a name for my new venture: Icebox Investigations. "So…I went to the office this morning and quit my job," I said. Surprised, everyone started to shift in their seats and look around the room at each other. I held my hands up. "Before you all say anything, consider this: I think I already have another case lined up."

My dad started nodding vigorously as I described the MIA inscription written on the wall of the Ainsley Mansion. "Is this what you and the other officer were talking about just before we all left?" he asked.

"Yep. He knew exactly what the inscription was: some kind of tribute to a woman and her newborn baby girl who vanished without a trace back in two thousand ten. Officer Hendricks really wants to be a detective, and I offered to help him investigate this case. If we can solve it, that might improve his chances." I shrugged. "I should know tomorrow if his leadership is on board with my proposal."

"And you think that getting in with the police department in River Junction might help us with the Fausts?" Kieran asked doubtfully.

"Je – I mean, Officer Hendricks did mention that they can't ever get charges against Edison to stick, not even, and I quote, 'when they beat an elderly couple to within an inch of their lives.' That makes me think they've had plenty of interactions with the Fausts over the years. He also said it's been really hard to hold them accountable for anything because the entire town is afraid of Edison. If I were a cop, that would be endlessly frustrating…and I might be a little more open to new and novel ways to put their asses in prison forever."

My dad was nodding again, and soon enough everyone was nodding with him. "It's worth a shot," Liam said. "That officer seems like a sharp fellow."

Hendricks' handsome face popped up in my mind's eye. Yes, he was indeed a sharp fellow. Then I thought of Nicholas and waited for the inevitable pang of guilt I always felt when I noticed a good-looking guy.

It never came.

∞

The family agreed that we would take turns keeping watch overnight, just in case. I was still pretty wound up, so I volunteered to take the first shift.

After everyone went to bed, I grabbed a blanket and my phone and curled up on one end of the couch under the glow of a table lamp. I opened the text messaging app on my phone and called up Nicholas' name. There was nothing more recent than the two texts he'd sent me on Thursday night. One said I was right. And the other said Call me. I'd been so inebriated when they came through that I forgot all about them until yesterday, when Mimi called me while I was up north after a close call with Morgan and an SUV in a supermarket parking lot.

I was deeply angry with Nicholas for not trying harder to get a hold of me after I didn't respond to these texts. I wanted to blame him for what happened to my dad, but in the darkness and quiet of the living room, it was difficult to ignore the fact that I was somewhat responsible too. I drank an entire bottle of chardonnay that Thursday night, for one. And, if I was being brutally honest, I'd been looking for reasons not to tell my family that Edison might have set his sights on us again because I didn't want to be forced to tell them how I knew.

I had selfishly put my family in harm's way to keep my relationship with Nicholas a secret.

I sighed. I was learning very quickly about the corrosive power of secrets. They dissolve relationships and destroy people as effectively as the strongest acid. And the secret I carried was causing me to make choices that had dire consequences. My dad was lucky this time...but what about next time? What if it was Mimi?

Tears burned behind my eyes as I stared at Nicholas' texts, trying to placate my guilty conscience. Suddenly a text notification popped up on the screen. It was from Nicholas, as if he knew I was thinking about him:

Hey babe. Look, I'm sorry if you think I did something wrong. Forgive me? Wanted to tell you I accessed E's computer remotely, and he's been looking at a lot of online auctions for gold coins. Not sure what that means. Call me when you get a chance. Love you.

My eyebrows drew together and my mood instantly flashed over from melancholy to enraged all over again. I re-read Nicholas' non-apology, then stabbed my phone's screen with a finger to close the text messaging app. I sighed deeply; things were fundamentally changing between Nicholas and me. I could feel it deep in my bones.

"Why the big sigh, sis?"

I jumped and dropped my phone in my lap, then looked up to see my brother making his way across the room toward me. "Jesus, Kieran, you scared the shit out of me."

"Sorry," he said. "Scootch."

I made room for him under my blanket, and he sat down next to me. Sitting together on the couch, sharing a blanket, brought back all the warm and fuzzy memories from our childhood. "Remember when we were little and we would sit right here, just like this, and watch TV while Dad was at work?"

Kieran chuckled. "Sometimes Mimi would make a fresh loaf of bread and bring some to us."

I closed my eyes; I could almost taste it. Mimi's homemade bread was always a staple in our house. The recipe was a closely-guarded secret, and I'd never been able to duplicate it. So I stopped trying, content to enjoy a fresh warm hunk of Mimi's bread lathered with creamy butter whenever I visited.

"Ah, the good old days," I said, and smiled.

"Those were the days I felt almost like a normal kid," Kieran said.

I knew exactly what he meant; our lives were turned upside down when our mother left. Nothing felt "normal" again after that. Dad and Mimi loved us and raised us as best they could – but there was no substitute for a mother's presence and love. I took his hand and squeezed it.

We sat in companionable silence for a minute or two, then he said, "Can I tell you something?"

"Of course."

"You are such a badass."

I blinked, surprised. "What do you mean?"

"Oh, stop playing dumb, Raegan. That was a gutsy move, showing up at the Ainsley Mansion and rescuing Dad. Where did you get that set of cast iron cajones?"

I chuckled. "Honestly, there wasn't a real plan or coherent thought. I was just running on sheer terror. Looking back, what I did was actually really stupid. I could have gotten us both killed."

"But you didn't," Kieran said. "You actually tried to do something. I've never seen anyone – not Mimi, not Dad, nobody – ever even attempt to stand up to the Fausts. We have our own personal boogeyman, and we never do anything but run and hide." His voice was bitter. "We might as well stand outside the Faust Fortress with a megaphone and shout 'Hey Edison! You missed again, haha! Better luck next time!'"

I thought about this for a second. "I think Mimi and Dad are just trying to live a normal life. You know? Not let fear of the Fausts rule us." As soon as I said this I knew how ridiculous it sounded.

"That's the problem," Kieran said. "It *does* rule us. Our lives – well, more your life than mine since Annie and I moved to Oregon – are *not* normal. Jesus Christ, Mimi sent Mom away because of that psychopath!"

I couldn't come up with an argument that made any sense, but I didn't really try that hard. My brother was absolutely right. And because we never fought back, Edison never had a reason not to keep trying to get his claws on our mother. Kieran and I had had this discussion numerous times over the years, but we could never get anywhere with Mimi. "Nobody knows how to handle the Fausts better than me," she would say. "You kids just do as I say and we'll be all right."

This time we came so close to not being all right. "I think what happened to Dad has really gotten to Mimi," I said. "She couldn't stop shaking earlier."

Kieran gazed at me with pale blue eyes just like my own. "Then maybe this is the time to think about changing our strategy for dealing with the Fausts," he said.

I held his gaze. "You want to bring Mom home, don't you?"

"Of course I do," he said fiercely. "And after she's home, we start fighting back."

"You do realize that the likelihood of Mimi agreeing to this is basically nonexistent, right?" I asked.

"Yes. But at what point do we decide that Mom and Dad and you and I are grown-ass adults who can make their own decisions?"

I winced at his brashness, but could not argue. "She's just trying to protect us, Kieran."

"I know, but her way isn't working anymore," he said. "It's time for a change."

I sighed. "All right. We'll talk to Dad and Mimi."

"Tomorrow."

I agreed.

Monday, July 12, 2021

CHAPTER 5

The persistent BUZZ of an incoming phone call drew me out of a deep sleep. My face felt hot. I breathed deeply through my nose and opened my eyes, only to squeeze them shut again against the bright morning sunlight pouring through the living room window and directly onto me. I was on the couch, covered with the blanket Kieran and I had shared the night before. I had fallen asleep and he left me where I lay rather than waking me to move me.

My phone buzzed again. I ran my hands over the blanket with my eyes still closed; finding nothing, I shaded my face with my hand to block the sunlight and turned to look over the edge of the couch. My phone lay on the hardwood floor, flashing Jesse Hendricks' name. I grabbed it and accepted the call.

"Good morning." My voice was gritty with sleep.

"Ms. O'Rourke? This is Officer Jesse Hendricks with the River Junction Police Department. I don't know if you remember, but –"

So formal, I thought. *After all we've been through together.* "Good morning," I repeated. "Of course I remember you. Hello. And please call me Raegan."

He faltered a bit, as if he had memorized a script and didn't know what to do because I wasn't following it. "Oh. Um, okay. Sorry. I – uh...I'm calling to follow up on our discussion yesterday."

"Okay." My gut churned – with excitement or dread, I couldn't quite tell.

"Yes." This made me smile. Hendricks had seemed pretty sure of himself in person yesterday; I wondered if he was always this adorably awkward on the phone, or if it was just me. "I spoke with my captain, and she is very interested in moving the Mia Masterson case off our books. She would be agreeable to bringing you on as a consultant to help investigate, but she wants to meet you first."

"Okay," I said again.

A clumsy pause, then: "Um, could you come now?"

"Oh!" I muscled myself up to a sitting position and slid my hand over my messy hair. I had no idea what time it was. "Uh, sure. I can be there in an hour."

"Okay," Hendricks said. "When you get here just give the lady at the desk your name, and she'll let you in."

"See you in a bit," I said, and rang off. I glanced at the clock on my way to the bathroom; it was ten o'clock and the house was silent. I showered and dressed in some of the extra clothes I kept in my childhood bedroom for unplanned sleepovers like this one. Back in the kitchen I scribbled a note telling my family where I'd be, grabbed my purse and my phone, and quietly left the house.

My heart twinged at the thought of leaving my family; would they be okay without me for a few hours?

I turned on the radio at low volume and let my thoughts wander as I drove up to River Junction. The morning show deejays on WWTH-FM - known colloquially as "The Hits" - were hamming it up, cracking jokes about celebrity mishaps and trying to stump each other with ridiculous trivia. After the hourly weather and traffic reports, lead deejay Matt Moe transitioned to his daily "News of the Weird" segment. I turned the volume up.

"Okay, guys, listen to this. This is just absolute craziness. Police in Nashville, Tennessee report that a thirty-five-year-old man was killed last week after a sinkhole opened under his house."

"Didn't that happen in Florida once?" This was a female deejay called Sarah Strange who sounded like she graduated from high school roughly fifteen minutes ago. "Like, a guy was sleeping and his whole bedroom just got sucked into a giant sinkhole?"

"Ohh yeahhh, I remember that." The morning show's producer, a velvet-voiced young man who simply went by G, chimed in. "Did they ever find his body?"

"Just wait, just wait, it gets better," Moe said. "The man, one Robert K. Martin, was sitting on...on the..." Moe couldn't finish his sentence. He was laughing too hard.

Sarah and G tried to coax more out of Moe. "Sitting on the what? Come on, Matt!"

Moe took a deep, heaving breath and managed to gain some control. "Mr. Martin was..." He couldn't contain a snort. "He was...ah, shall we say, attending to the call of nature when the unfortunate incident occurred."

Uncharacteristic silence in the studio as Sarah Strange and G processed this. Then G said tentatively, "Um, does that mean he was…he was pooping?"

Sarah gasped. "Oh my god, he was *pooping* when the sinkhole swallowed him up?"

Moe blew a long snorty laugh out through his nose behind Sarah, and then all three deejays erupted into hysterical guffaws, hoots and hollers. I laughed right along with them. I couldn't help it. The poor schmuck lost his life in such a dramatic way while doing something so mundane. It was comedy gold.

Moe managed to regain enough control to finish his report. "Mr. Martin's body, along with his toilet, are buried so far underground that officials don't believe they'll ever be able to recover him." Another snort. "This radio show hopes Mr. Martin rests in peace."

The morning show crew moved on to their next topic, and I turned off the radio just as I crossed the Mississippi River into River Junction. I glanced briefly down River Street as I drove past on Bridge Street, remembering the events of the day before and feeling grateful that my dad and I got out of the Ainsley Mansion alive.

I was going to stop Edison Faust. One way or another.

I turned right onto Greenhaven Road and pulled into the parking lot of the boxy red brick building that housed the River Junction Police Department. The officer at the front desk, the name SOLOMON embroidered on her chest, had a severe square face and wore her brown hair pulled back into a tight bun. She looked like she hadn't cracked a smile in at least a decade. She buzzed the heavy steel door open and led me into the bowels of the police station.

"Have a seat," she pointed to a smallish waiting area outside a set of offices. "I'll let Jesse know you're here."

"Thank you," I said and sat in a wood-framed chair upholstered in an excruciatingly ugly 1970s shade of dark brown.

Officer Solomon smiled, and her entire face changed. *She's actually quite pretty*, I thought. She turned and went back to her post.

I fidgeted with my gloves while I waited, pulling them partly off and then all the way back on to my hands. Jesse Hendricks rounded a corner; he wore his full patrol uniform and seemed stiff and uncomfortable compared to yesterday. "Ms. O'Rourke?"

I stood. "Hello. Please, call me Raegan." *What is it with these law enforcement guys?* I wondered, remembering how long it took Chad Overton to get comfortable calling me by my first name.

A halting smile crossed Hendricks' clean-shaven face. "Okay. Sorry," he said. "Follow me, I'll take you to my captain's office."

My eyes roved over Hendricks' entire back side as I followed him. He was tall and muscular, his shoulders wide, his butt firm. His back was straight, and he wore the uniform and the heavily laden belt like he was born for it. He had a red birthmark vaguely shaped like the state of Illinois on the nape of his neck, just above his collar. For the briefest moment I envisioned myself touching that sensitive spot with my bare fingers. I wondered what I would see.

I shook my head and tried to replace those thoughts with a mental picture of Nicholas. It was harder than I expected it would be. When I finally envisaged Nicholas' pale face and huge black eyes framed by a shock of wild black hair, it didn't elicit the same reaction in me that Hendricks' back had.

Hendricks approached the open door of a large office; the name on the plate mounted on the sidelight was CAPT. SARAH BAILEY. He stood aside to let me enter first.

A petite Asian woman in a basic cop-boss pantsuit stood behind a standard-issue corporate desk and watched us walk in. I didn't really know what to expect when I entered, but I certainly didn't expect Captain Sarah Bailey. She was *tiny*, for one thing; I would have been shocked if she measured a full five feet tall. Hendricks towered over her. She was also stunningly beautiful; if she'd been half a foot taller, she could have had a heck of a modeling career. Her straight black hair was cut shoulder-length with bangs that brushed her almond-shaped eyes. This woman oversaw the entire patrol division of the River Junction Police Department, reporting directly to the Chief of Police – which made her the supervisor of a couple dozen people. *She's the one with the cast-iron cajones,* I thought. *I would do well to stay on her good side.*

Bailey's office was large, with plenty of room for a desk and a small conference table that could seat four people. A good-sized window overlooked a lush green courtyard and let in plenty of sunlight. A framed photo of Bailey with a younger teenage girl who looked just like her sat on the desk next to the computer monitor; beyond that there were no other decorations. Not even an inspirational quote or a potted plant.

I stood awkwardly in an open space between the table and the door while Hendricks introduced me. "Captain, this is Raegan O'Rourke, the lady I was telling you about."

Bailey rounded her desk with her hand extended. I shook it and noticed her noticing my gloves. "Ms. O'Rourke, it's a pleasure." Her accentless voice was much deeper than I'd expected for someone so petite.

"Likewise," I said. "You can call me Raegan."

Bailey gestured toward the conference table. "Please, have a seat. Would you like anything to drink?"

"No thank you, I'm fine," I said and sat at the table. Hendricks also declined her offer and sat next to me.

Bailey took a third seat and crossed her perfect little legs. "Well then, let's get right to it, shall we? Officer Hendricks says you might be able to help us with one of our more vexing cold cases. I assume he filled you in on the details?"

"He did, and I believe I can help. I'd love the opportunity to try."

"Mia Masterson and her baby have been missing for almost eleven years," she said. "Vanished without a trace. No clues, no leads, no financial activity, no sightings. Nothing. We keep the case open as a formality, but the prevailing opinion in this department for the last decade has been that it cannot be solved." She held my gaze. "How do you think you can solve an unsolvable case?"

My heart quickened. "I have a couple tools in my proverbial toolbox," I said. "The first is, I have ten years of experience as an investigative reporter for the Minneapolis Daily News & Review. I'm not afraid to talk to people, and I'm certainly not afraid to ask tough questions. I believe someone out there knows something. I will track them down and I will get the information we need to find Mia and her baby.

"Second, I very recently – like, two days ago – solved a cold case not unlike this one. My neighbors lost their dog when the lake resort cabin they were staying in burned to the ground. I wanted to help them find out why. Sort of, you know, supplement law enforcement's investigation into the cause of the fire." I did not mention that I was going to use my touch to do it. "So I went up north and stayed at the same resort and started asking around. I stumbled across the cold case of two teenagers who went missing from that very resort twenty-five years ago."

Bailey's and Hendricks' eyes were trained on me. "And?" Bailey asked.

I smiled. "That case was as ice cold as Mia Masterson's. It hadn't moved in *years*. Those kids vanished without a trace and there were no leads, even after several big searches. They were just…gone. I managed to convince Kabetogama County Sheriff Chad Overton to let me help. We investigated, and within a week I had it solved. I figured out who burned the cabin down, too, and why."

Bailey gave a small smile. "A twofer. Impressive."

"There's one more thing," Hendricks interjected. "Raegan here has a gift. A gift that could come in very handy with this case."

Shit. I turned and glared at Hendricks. He threw me a quick apologetic glance.

"Oh? And what is that?" Bailey looked at me brightly.

You're gonna pay for this, Hendricks, I thought and clenched my teeth. "I don't know if I'd call it a gift so much. It's more of an ability. You know." I hoped my dismissive tone would encourage Bailey to change the subject.

Instead she raised her perfectly sculpted eyebrows.

I didn't want to say more, but her expression compelled me. "It's, ah....well, it's a psychic ability." I sighed, trying to ignore Mimi's long-ago voice in my head saying *Everything will be fine as long as you keep your touch a secret.* "I can touch a thing and see visions of events that happened to or near that thing in the past."

Bailey's face did not change, except for one long, slow blink. "Excuse me?"

"It's true, Captain," Hendricks cut in again. "Her family is legacy River Junction and their abilities are well known here."

A vertical line formed between Bailey's eyebrows, but the rest of her face remained stoic.

"The Ainsleys?" Hendricks said hopefully.

Bailey blinked again, this time in shock, and sat back in her chair. "You're an Ainsley? Is that why you wear those gloves?"

I nodded.

"There hasn't been an Ainsley living in River Junction since before World War Two, but this town has a long memory." Hendricks said.

"Edison Faust doesn't forget, either." The vertical line was back between her eyebrows as she gazed at me. "I read Officer Hendricks' report this morning about your...encounter with him yesterday."

I looked down at my gloved hands and remembered Hendricks saying *The fact that you had a gun and fired it at Edison and Morgan opens you up to assault charges as well.*

"I'm going to have a talk with the county attorney and persuade him that you shot at Morgan and Edison Faust in self-defense." Bailey leaned her elbows on the table and looked at

Hendricks, her voice bitter. "We both know they'll never see a charge for kidnapping and assaulting Mr. O'Rourke, so..." She left her sentence unfinished, but I caught her unspoken meaning: *There's no sense in charging you, either.* I was grateful, and I said so. And although I wanted to know more about why the Fausts were so rarely held accountable for their crimes, I decided now was not the right time to ask. It would all come in due time. First I had to get the gig.

Bailey waved off my thanks. "It's the right thing to do. Besides, I can't have my first contract detective under investigation while she's working for me."

I stared at her blankly for a second; when I realized what she'd said, my whole body jerked in my chair. "Oh! Does that mean – ?"

"I believe you have the experience and the unique perspective this department needs to bring resolution to Mia Masterson's case. I actually spoke to Chad Overton just before you arrived, and he sings your praises. Told me you were our only hope for solving the Mia Masterson case and I'd be a damn fool if I didn't bring you on."

I smiled and shook my head. *That sounds like my lumberjack sheriff.* "Thank you, Captain."

"You'll report to me while on assignment with us, but Detective Sergeant Carter Rooney will be your day-to-day supervisor." Bailey turned her attention to Hendricks. "The same goes for you, Jesse. I'm moving you to a special assignment with the Investigations unit so you can work the Mia Masterson case and Raegan here can shadow you. Officer Chase will partner with Officer Lopez for the time being."

"Yes, ma'am."

We discussed the administrative details, and then Bailey stood. Hendricks and I followed suit. "I'll have Amy, our City Manager, prepare the paperwork. I imagine it'll be ready for your signature tomorrow."

"Thank you," I said, and extended my hand.

Bailey shook it. "Glad to have you here, Raegan. I'm looking forward to finding out what happened to Mia Masterson. We all are." Something else occurred to her. "Oh. One last thing. There's an empty office you can use while you're here. Both of you. You'll find the case files waiting for you there."

Hendricks and I thanked Captain Bailey again and made our way to our new war room. I felt like I was floating. I couldn't believe my good fortune.

Icebox Investigations had its very first case.

CHAPTER 6

The office wasn't nearly as large as Captain Bailey's, but it would do just fine. Two file storage boxes sat on the desk; they each had MASTERSON and a 2010 case number scrawled on them in black marker. A big whiteboard hung on the wall.

"Welcome to the River Junction Police Department, Ms. O — I mean, Raegan," Hendricks said, his green eyes bright. He was as excited as I was; he'd just scored his ticket to the promotion he so badly wanted. "Let's solve us a cold case."

I set my purse on the desk, sat in a chair, and pulled a box toward me. "No reason we can't get started now, is there?"

"Let's do it." Hendricks started to sit in the other chair, then changed his mind and went to the whiteboard instead. He selected a red marker and wrote MIA MASTERSON in the top center of the board, then faced me. "Let's map out what we know so we can see what gaps we have."

"Good call," I said. "Then we'll review the case files and hopefully fill in some of those gaps. After that we'll have a pretty good idea of where to start."

"Right." Hendricks turned back to the board and wrote in bold capital letters as he talked. "So we know that Mia and Isabel disappeared early the morning of September twenty-second, two thousand ten. Uh. She was driving a black Jeep Liberty. Mia was twenty-eight years old at the time, and Isabel was four days old. They had just been released from Oakview Hospital the day before." The marker's felt tip pounded and squeaked almost frantically against the board's shiny white surface. He stopped and stared at the ceiling for a moment, thinking, then continued. "She lived alone. The original investigation didn't turn up a partner, and it is unknown who Isabel's father is." He drew a big question mark next to Isabel Masterson's name.

"I gotta believe someone out there knows who the baby's father is," I pointed out. "Who did the original investigators talk to?"

Hendricks gestured at the file boxes. "We'll have to look in the files, but I do know they spoke with a neighbor."

"Okay. What else do we know?"

Hendricks recapped the marker. "Those are the basics off the top of my head."

"Let's see what the files say." We took the lids off the boxes. My box contained manila folders stuffed with papers, but at first glance I didn't see any photographs. I realized I had no idea what our missing person looked like. "Do we have a photo of Mia?"

"Ah, good question." Hendricks dug through his files until he found a manila folder with Mia's name on it. He glanced inside and then handed it to me. I flipped it open to reveal a photo of a pretty woman with pixie-cut dark brown hair, big brown eyes, and a wide smile. She leaned against a bar, grinning and holding a shot glass up as if toasting the photographer. She wore black pants, a black t-shirt, and a black server's apron. I showed the photo to Hendricks. "Looks like she worked at a bar or restaurant."

"She worked at two, actually." He took the photo, examined it, and then stuck it to the board with tape scrounged from a desk drawer. "I know one was the Rummery, that's a couple blocks from here. I don't recall what the other one was."

I skimmed Mia's file. "The Majestic Saloon," I read.

"Ah, yes. River Junction's oldest bar. It's been around since the eighteen-seventies." Hendricks wrote the names of the bars on the whiteboard.

I looked through the rest of the papers in Mia's folder and pulled out a typed report. I skimmed it as I spoke. "It says here that Mia's neighbor's name was James Locke." I spelled it for him so he could write that on the board too. "He saw Mia loading the baby into her car around seven forty-five in the morning. She was wearing black yoga pants and a white cropped shirt. She drove away, headed south on Fourth Avenue."

More pounds and squeaks from Hendricks' whiteboard marker. "Seven forty-five," he muttered.

My eyes followed my finger down the page. "Ah, let's see what else — oh. She rented a house across the street from James. A fellow named Alex Blackett was her landlord."

"I know that guy. He was three or four years ahead of me in high school. Played football and basketball, thought he was pretty hot shit. Now he lives in his dad's house and is a custodian at the hospital." Hendricks wrote Blackett's name on the board.

"That's all that was in that report." I set the paper aside and paged through Mia's folder again, looking for a report that documented a conversation with Alex Blackett. I came across a thick stack of papers that had been clipped together. "Jesse," I said. "I have her cell phone records."

Hendricks recapped the marker and pulled the second chair closer to me. He smelled really nice, like a beach sunrise. We sat shoulder-to-shoulder and tried to make sense of the densely packed letters and numbers that covered both sides of all thirty or so pages. Some numbers were highlighted in yellow, but I couldn't discern a pattern to help me understand why.

Hendricks blew air out between his lips. "There must be months' worth of phone calls here."

I flipped to the last page. The final entry was highlighted in yellow. Mia had made a brief call to the Junction Medical Clinic at 8:17 the morning she disappeared. "Okay," I said, and sat back in my chair. "So James Locke saw Mia at seven forty-five, and she made her last call at eight-seventeen."

Hendricks stood and added this information to the impressive diagram he had constructed on the whiteboard. It was nice to have a visual of all the players and key information to help keep the facts of the case straight. "Do we know where she was during those thirty-two minutes?" he asked.

"I haven't seen anything." I looked closer at the cell records and realized with dismay that text messages were not included. I could see how many she'd sent (1,238) but not what they said or who she sent them to. "What — how are there no texts in here?"

"Maybe they're separate from the phone records." Hendricks said hopefully. We combed through both boxes and came up empty. Mia's case files were in better shape than the Catclaw Kids' had been, but they were not as thorough as I'd expected. *Mia deserved better than this,* I thought, and asked Hendricks his opinion.

He nodded. "I don't know if Detective Baker gave up or what, but it doesn't look like Mia was a priority for him. I remember he retired from the department like six months after Mia disappeared, so maybe he just didn't give a shit." He shook his head sadly. "I'll talk to Sergeant Rooney about subpoenaing Mia's text messages."

"Or maybe Baker didn't even think to request text records," I said, then something occurred to me. "Who reported her missing?" I asked.

"Ah…" Hendricks dug through the piles of paper on the desk in front of him and produced a missing persons report. "Looks like it was Alex Blackett."

I skimmed the report. "This is dated September twenty-fifth. She was missing for three days before he realized it?"

Hendricks held my gaze. "I guess we should go talk to him, huh?"

"Yep. And James Locke too."

We spent the next hour or two like that, reviewing documents and making sense of Mia's case. Conversation with Jesse Hendricks was remarkably easy, like we'd known each other for twenty-four years and not just twenty-four hours.

I pulled my purse toward me and looked at my phone. My heart dropped when I saw it was nearing three o'clock. I hadn't planned to be away from my family for this long. I took a deep breath to steady my heart and my hands. "Let's plan to visit Alex Blackett and James Locke tomorrow morning, okay?"

"Sure. Everything all right?" His bright green eyes watched my face closely, and I knew he could see my worry.

"I guess I'm still jumpy after the encounter with Edison and Morgan Faust yesterday. I really want to get home and make sure my family is okay."

"Okay. We'll meet back here tomorrow at oh-eight-hundred hours."

"Thanks." I gathered my things and headed for the door. His voice stopped me just before I stepped out into the hall.

"Raegan?"

I turned. "Yeah?"

"Thank you." He smiled, and his face transformed from the serious face of a cop who had seen too many bad things to that of a fresh-faced teenager, vibrant and ready to take on the world. *I bet that's what his senior high school photo looks like*, I thought.

"This case really means a lot. I think we'll make a great team." I gave him a quick wave and ducked out into the hall.

CHAPTER 7

My car's tires screeched as I turned into my dad's driveway and parked. The house was still standing, although that didn't mean that Edison and Morgan Faust hadn't already been here and exacted their revenge. Mental pictures of my family killed in every gory and bloody way paraded through my head as I burst through the door. I was so wound up that when I came upon Mimi in the kitchen making dinner, her face was covered in blood and some of it dripped off her chin and into the alfredo sauce she was stirring with a gloved hand.

Luckily the scream lodged in my throat and stayed there, because when she turned and smiled at me, the blood was gone and her face was as lovable and careworn as ever. I took a deep breath and willed my heart to slow down.

"Hi, love." Mimi's gaze lingered on my face. "Are you all right?"

Another cleansing breath. "Yeah, I'm okay. I was just worried. You know."

Mimi nodded. "No Faust sightings today."

"Where is everyone?" I opened the fridge and found a half-full bottle of chardonnay. I didn't know how old it was, and I didn't really care; a glass of wine, even wine that was on its way to vinegar, was exactly what I needed right now. I ignored Mimi's disapproving eyes boring holes into my back as I poured a glass.

"Your father decided to brave the office today," Mimi said, turning back to the stove. "And Kieran took Annie to the airport."

"Why?" I took a sip. The wine was fine, crisp and cold and delicious like an apple.

"He decided she would be safer back in Oregon. He's going to stay for a while longer."

"Okay." I was sad that Annie had left, but could not argue with my brother's logic. She probably was safer in Eugene. The kitchen smelled amazing, and I moved closer to the stove. "What's for dinner?"

"Your dad asked for chicken alfredo. Now shoo – it'll be ready in a bit."

I shooed, making my way to the three-season porch that looked out on the backyard. This was my dad's favorite spot in the whole house, with its full roof and the floor-to-ceiling screened windows that comprised three walls. The patio furniture was covered in thick, fluffy cushions, throw pillows, and blankets, all of which could easily be stashed in the weatherproof chest that doubled as a coffee table. Faux ficus trees stood in every corner, and string lights hung loosely overhead. The giant oak trees in my dad's backyard provided ample shade, and the screens allowed the breeze to keep the room cool. A large framed photo of my mother, her curly blonde hair wild and her laughing face full of joy, hung on the wall next to the sliding door that led to the house. I wanted to curl up on the loveseat out there and just sit; I'd taken in a lot of information today, and I needed some quiet time to process it.

My phone buzzed just as I sat down. It was a text from Aaron Long, my next-door neighbor. I hadn't been to my condo since I arrived home yesterday morning after resigning from my job to find the place ransacked and a threatening note from Morgan Faust stuck to the wall with my butcher knife. I'd left in a panic, not bothering to close the door behind me. Hi Raegan, I noticed your door was open, so I peeked inside. I think you've been burglarized. Are you ok? Please let me know, Kellie and I are worried. I'll call the police if I don't hear back from you in 30 minutes.

I winced, and guilt panged deep in my gut. Aaron and his wife Kellie were the neighbors who had been staying at Wanderer's Resort when their cabin mysteriously burned down on the Fourth of July, taking Baxter, their beloved Cocker Spaniel, with it. My joy at discovering the how and why behind Baxter's senseless death had swiftly been tempered by Edison Faust's latest antics, and soon enough my entire focus was on my family and not on my condo or my amazing neighbors. I would be staying at my dad's for the foreseeable future, and if I were even a halfway decent neighbor and friend, I would have let Aaron and Kellie know. I set my glass on the table and typed out a reply. Hi Aaron, I'm fine. No need to call the police. I know my place is a mess, but I promise I wasn't burglarized. It's a long story. I'm staying at my dad's for a while, family stuff, but I'll keep in touch. Thanks for checking on me.

I hit send, picked my glass up, and sank into the thick cushions of the loveseat. It was a lovely late afternoon, relatively cool for mid-July, and the shadows of the trees were growing longer on my dad's carefully tended lawn. I watched two robins hop around the lush grass in search of worms, listened to a very vocal cardinal sing from a nearby tree branch, and sipped my wine. My brain and my body finally started to relax, allowing the cluttered thoughts in my brain to sort themselves out.

Someone out there knows what happened to Mia Masterson. My money's on the landlord. What's his name...Alex? Yeah, Alex. I bet he knows something. I mean, who waits three days to report someone missing? Totally suspicious.

Jesse has a really nice smile. I could almost see myself kissing those lips. Ugh. Stop it, O'Rourke. Nicholas is the love of my life, remember? And for all I know, Jesse is happily married. Did I see a ring? I don't know. Note to self, look for one tomorrow.

Nicholas. When did I last talk to Nicholas? I should probably call him. We've been through a lot in the last eleven years, I'm sure we can work all this out with a simple conversa–

"Hey."

My thought cut cleanly off and my entire body jerked, sending the last bit of wine out of my glass and onto my shirt. I gave Kieran the stink eye as he sat in the chair next to me. "Jesus Christ, you scared the shit out of me."

"Sorry," he said, not looking sorry at all. "What have you been up to today?"

"I spent most of the day in River Junction." I told him about meeting Captain Sarah Bailey and getting the green light to work the Mia Masterson case with Jesse Hendricks.

"That's awesome, Rae," he said, smiling. "I know this is a big deal for you."

"Thanks." I sat up and set my empty wine glass on the table. My body was warm and relaxed – the first stage of the perfect buzz. I knew I should stop now. I also knew I probably wouldn't. I was already thinking about another glass. "I'm sorry to hear Annie went home."

"She didn't want to." He looked morose. "I told her I couldn't let her become a victim of Edison Faust's. I'd never be able to live with myself if something happened to her and I could have prevented it."

It was the same reason I had basically no friends. I was careful to keep people at arm's length to protect them from my real-life boogeyman. "You should go home too, Kieran. Be with your wife and keep yourself safe."

"You're out of your mind if you think I'm going to do that, Rae. I meant what I said last night. I want to bring Mom home and take Edison Faust down." He took a deep breath. "I will go back to Oregon when I know for sure my family is safe."

I didn't have anything to say to that, so I reached over and grasped his hand. "O'Rourke to the rescue, right?" This was his catchphrase anytime we played superheroes as kids. He always got to be the dashing figure with a tablecloth for a cape, and I always had to be the damsel in distress. My pleas to be a superhero too – hell, I would have even settled for sidekick – fell on deaf ears. "I need someone to rescue, Rae," he would say. "Okay?"

He grinned, and then he laughed. "That's right. O'Rourke to the rescue."

I smiled and squeezed his hand, feeling the love for my big brother.

He squeezed back. "Still up for talking to Dad and Mimi about Mom?"

My stomach felt funny. "Yeah. I'm worried about what Mimi will say, though. I don't–"

"What Mimi will say about what?" There she stood in the doorway to the house, resplendent in her loud floral apron and the yellow latex gloves she always wore while cooking.

"How long have you been standing there?" I demanded.

"Just long enough to hear you say you're worried about what I'll say. Come inside, let's talk about it over dinner."

Kieran and I looked at each other, gave identical sighs, and stood. "Is it possible that she already knows?" I said, picking my wine glass up from the table.

"Of course it's possible," Kieran said as he followed me inside. "I'm pretty sure she knows everything."

I stopped in the kitchen to refill my glass, then joined my family at the dining room table. Liam sat in his customary spot at the head of the table. The wound on his forehead was completely scabbed over and the bruise around it was still pretty dark – but he was in good spirits. Mimi's chair was at the foot of the table closest to the kitchen, and Kieran and I sat on either side, facing each other. Mimi had placed large glasses filled with ice water in front of each seat; I set my wine glass next to my water glass and looked greedily at the food. My mouth would not stop watering. Steaming bowls of linguine noodles and creamy homemade alfredo sauce, along with plates of pan-fried chicken strips and gooey cheesy garlic bread, covered the table. Mimi appeared from the kitchen with a giant glass bowl filled to the brim with fresh green salad. She set the bowl in the middle of the table and took her seat.

"All right." She gestured at the feast before her. "Dig in."

We caught each other up on the day's activities as we passed dishes and loaded our plates. I told them about River Junction PD taking me on and what I'd learned about the Mia Masterson case so far. My dad and Mimi congratulated me just as Kieran had.

Kieran told my dad about sending Annie home. Liam somberly slathered the pile of linguine noodles on his plate with alfredo sauce. "I'm sorry to hear that," he said. "But it is probably for the best." He wound a bit of pasta around his fork and took a bite. "This is delicious, Emily."

He was right. The alfredo pasta was warm and creamy and full of flavor, and I never wanted it to end.

Mimi dipped her head and forked some salad into her mouth. She chewed for a few seconds, then said, "Thank you, Liam." She washed it down with some water and then pointed her fork at me. "No more small talk, now. What were you kids talking about on the porch?"

Butterflies fluttered in my gut; I tried to drown them with a large gulp of wine. Then I opened my mouth to speak.

Kieran beat me to it. "We want to talk about Mom."

Mimi's head swiveled and she regarded him for a beat. "All right."

"We'd like to talk about bringing her home," I chimed in, sounding much braver than I felt. My insides quivered.

Mimi's head turned back to me; she looked like she was watching a tennis match. Then she faced forward and sent Liam a meaningful look. Kieran and I both looked at him.

"What?" Kieran said.

"What's going on?" I asked.

"Ah, well." Dad lifted the napkin from his lap and used it to dab the wrinkled corners of his mouth. "Your grandmother and I have been discussing that very idea for a while now."

My eyes widened. Kieran's did too. I looked back at Mimi to make sure I'd heard my dad correctly. "Is that true?"

Mimi held her hands up in front of her. "Nothing's been decided."

I stared at Mimi, gobsmacked. *All these years,* I thought, anxiety morphing into indignation, even anger, in my gut. "All these years you wouldn't even entertain the idea of bringing Mom home. And now…"

Kieran's face looked like my insides felt. "What changed? And when were you going to tell us?"

Liam laid his napkin across his lap and cleared his throat. "Well, before yesterday, it had been a long time since we'd seen or heard from Edison Faust or anyone in his family. We were hopeful that perhaps there wasn't so much of a threat anymore, and that maybe it was finally safe enough for your mom to come home."

"In fact," Mimi chimed in, "I'm not convinced it's a good idea. Not at all. *Especially* after what happened yesterday." She blinked furiously. For a moment I wondered if she had something in her eye, and then I realized she was trying to hold back tears. My heart broke a little.

"Mimi," Kieran said gently. "It's time. She – really, all of us – *we* can't live in fear forever."

Mimi's face crumpled, and she bowed her head.

Kieran's eyes burned. "Rae and I have been talking, and we really believe that with Mom here with us, we'll be better able to defend ourselves. We might even be able to take Edison Faust and his family down."

"We're stronger together," I said. "Especially with our touch, Mimi."

"They have a point, Emily," Liam said. "I –"

Mimi slammed her fists down on the table, rattling dishes and making us all jump. "Don't you people understand? I almost lost her once!" Mimi's chest heaved, and tears flowed freely down her cheeks. Her eyes blazed. "Edison came this close to taking my daughter, my only child, away from me! I – I can't…" She covered her face with her hands.

"Thirty-two years, Mimi." My broken heart rattled in my chest, and tears burned behind my eyes.

"That's a long time for this family to live without a daughter, wife, and mother." Kieran's face was streaked with tears.

We all sat in silence for several minutes while the delicious food went cold in front of us. Mimi's sobs gradually became ragged breaths and hiccups, and finally she removed her gloved hands from her red, blotchy face. Never in my life had I seen my Mimi so upset.

"Emily." My dad broke the tense silence. "I think you know that it's time to bring Danielle home."

Mimi's head was bowed, and she appeared to be studying her hands. Then she sighed and looked up with red-rimmed eyes.

"I'm scared," she said. Her voice was reedy and thin, like the voice of a much older woman.

"We're all scared, Mimi. We have allowed Edison Faust to terrorize our family for entirely too long," Kieran said, taking Mimi's hand. "It's time to take that power away from him. No more living in fear, Mimi. Wouldn't that be nice?"

"How?" Mimi's moist eyes were at the same time hopeful and doubtful. "How do we do that?"

"We don't know yet, exactly," I said. "But the first step is to bring Mom home, where she belongs."

"And we'll figure out the rest," Kieran added. "Raegan has an in with the River Junction Police Department now. Maybe that'll be our ticket to freedom from the Fausts."

There was one more possibility, one that wild horses would never drag out of me: Nicholas. Although at that moment I wasn't sure whose side Nicholas was on.

I had one burning question I'd never been able to get a straight answer for; now seemed like as good a time as any to ask again. "Where is she, Mimi? Where has Mom been all this time?"

Mimi looked like she had aged ten years in the last hour. Resigned, she tipped her chin toward my dad. "You tell them, Liam."

Dad cleared his throat. "Do you two remember Uncle Carl?"

Kieran and I nodded in unison. Carl Engelman was the former husband of Liam's sister and only sibling, Deirdre O'Rourke Engelman. They divorced when I was in high school, and I hadn't seen "Uncle Carl" since…but I never forgot his head, its shiny and hairless crown ringed with fine tawny hair on the back and sides. His lush mustache was thicker than the hair on his head.

"He owns a small cabin deep in the woods up north, not too far from the north shore of Lake Superior. About forty miles north of Duluth. The cabin and the land have been in his family for generations. It's so remote that the road to the cabin, really it's more of a path, is impassable in the winter without a snowmobile. The nearest town is about ten miles away."

I glanced at Kieran; the dumbfounded expression on his face matched the feeling in my gut. "Um, so you took her up to the middle of the northwoods and just left her there in a remote cabin all by herself?" I pictured my beautiful and vibrant mother living off the land and off the grid like some doomsday hermit. This was far worse than anything I'd ever imagined growing up.

"Like, does she have indoor plumbing?" Kieran asked. "Electricity? Heat? A freaking refrigerator?"

"A car?" I chimed in.

Liam held his hands up again. "Yes, yes. Your mother has electricity, heat, a full kitchen, and plumbing. She has a car and a snowmobile. She goes to town and buys gas and groceries. She has a phone and internet service."

Silence filled the room as my brother and I stared at our father in complete disbelief. "All these ways to leave a footprint, and you never worried that Edison Faust would find her?" Kieran nearly spat the words out.

"None of it is under her name. Or ours. Carl has been very accommodating, making sure your mother is well taken care of up there."

"If she had the ability to stay in touch, why didn't she?" I couldn't keep the tremble out of my voice. Something inside me felt fragile, like even the slightest breath might shatter it into a thousand shards.

"We couldn't take the chance," Mimi said. "Especially when you two were younger, we couldn't risk you telling your friends or teachers where your mother was."

"You didn't trust us," Kieran muttered. His anger had morphed into a powerful sadness I could feel from across the table.

"We were protecting your mother," Liam said. He glanced at Mimi. "In hindsight, we probably could have handled it differently."

The fragile thing inside me suddenly exploded, and I abruptly stood. Dishes, glasses, and silverware rattled when my leg thudded against the edge of the dining table. "You think?" I shouted. I looked wildly back and forth at my grandmother and my father. "You hid our mother from us for thirty fucking *years!* Do you two have any idea the damage you've done?" My heart quivered and I couldn't catch my breath; I had to leave (*right now*) before I said or did something I couldn't take back. I threw my napkin on top of my forgotten plate of alfredo and rushed out of the dining room.

"Raegan!" Mimi called after me. I retrieved my purse and left the house, heading straight for my car. I didn't know where I would go.

At that point I didn't really care.

CHAPTER 8

The sun was low on the horizon, at just the right angle to render both my sunglasses and my car's sun visor useless. So I kept my vehicle pointed south and east as much as possible. I wasn't sure I would pass a breath test if I got pulled over, so I drove extra carefully and about five miles per hour slower than I normally would to avoid suspicion.

The hustle and bustle of the city gave way to the wide streets of the suburbs, and then the relative tranquility of the exurbs. I left the radio turned off and drove in silence, letting my brain work its way through all the stuff.

First on my mind: it occurred to me that if my dad was telling the truth, and I had no reason to believe he wasn't, I had been less than a two hours' drive from my mother during the few days I spent at Wanderer's Resort. The thought made me want to cry and throw up at the same time. *I was so close,* I thought.

Then my thoughts veered to my Mimi. I'd never understood why she'd felt the need to do something so drastic as to hide my mother away from everyone, including her own children. I knew that Edison Faust wanted control of Mom's touch, but even the threat of a sneak attack had never stopped the rest of us from going about our lives. Why did my mom have to sacrifice so much more than everyone else?

At dinner Mimi had said *I almost lost her once!* and *Edison came this close to taking my daughter, my only child, away from me!* I wondered what had happened. What terrible thing did Edison Faust do that made hiding my mother in a remote cabin deep in the northwoods of Minnesota an attractive proposition?

Whatever it was, Mimi had never breathed even a hint of it to me. Or to Kieran, as far as I knew. *She really is a master at keeping secrets,* I thought.

My thoughts segued to Nicholas, and guilt panged in my gut. *I guess I learned how to keep a secret from the best.* Then, as if he knew I was thinking about him, my phone rang and his number popped up on my SUV's console screen. I gritted my teeth and accepted the call. "Hey."

"Hey back." Nicholas' deep honey voice filled my car. "Ah, you didn't respond to my text, thought I'd check in."

My peripheral vision briefly flashed red. *Oh, so NOW you follow up on an unanswered text,* I thought. I took a deep breath to calm myself. "Sorry, I've been busy."

"How is the family? Is your dad okay?"

Something in his voice stopped me from giving him an honest answer. I realized with growing sadness that for the first time in the whole of our relationship, I didn't completely trust him. *Oh, this is bad,* I thought. Something really had changed between us, and the churning deep in my gut was proof.

"He's fine."

"All right, if you say so. How are you?"

"I'm fine."

A moment of silence, then: "Is something wrong?"

My peripheral vision flashed red again. *As if you don't know.* "Everything's fine. What's up?"

"Did you see my text?"

"I did," I confirmed. The county road I was driving on had led me out of the Twin Cities and into rural farmland. My headlights popped on, illuminating corn and bean fields on either side of the road and reflecting off the huge eyes of some animal crouching in the ditch. *Raccoon?* I wondered.

"Edison would kill me–" I knew this was not an exaggeration "–if he knew I remotely accessed his computer and looked through his browser history, but I thought it was worth the risk. That *you* were worth the risk."

"Okay." Nicholas was trying to get back in my good graces. I was going to make him work for it.

"I mentioned he's been looking at online auctions for gold coins. He's also been doing daily searches for gold prices." He paused. "It's almost $1,800 an ounce right now."

I gave a low whistle. "Holy shit."

"Right? The thing is, I don't know *why* he's looking at gold prices. I can make an educated guess that he has some plan to acquire gold using your mother, and then sell it, but I don't know the specifics."

"Can you find out for me? Please? It's really important." I thought about my family's dinner conversation; if Edison actually had a coherent plan that could end up making him a very wealthy man, we might want to reconsider the timing of our plan to bring Mom home. Sending her into hiding sucked for the family, but was so far one hundred percent effective in keeping her out of

Edison Faust's evil clutches. With that much money on the line, he would never stop until he had her.

We would all do well to watch our backs. I sighed.

"Of course. I'll let you know as soon as I know something. I promise." I heard a note of contrition in his voice.

Suddenly I was deeply, bone-crushingly tired – the kind of exhaustion that comes after days of riding an emotional rollercoaster. "I have to go. I'll talk to you later."

"Okay. I lo–"

I ended the call, not in any mood to hear that or spend any more emotional capital thinking about Nicholas. It was time to go home.

∞

I dragged myself into the darkened house, ready to fall into bed. I had to be in River Junction by eight o'clock tomorrow morning – *oh-eight-hundred hours,* Jesse Hendricks had said – and I needed sleep.

The fates had other plans. I glanced into the living room on my way by and saw Mimi sitting on the couch with the old Ainsley family scrapbook on her lap. A knot formed in my gut as I changed course and went to sit next to her.

"I'm sorry, Mimi." Tears effervesced behind my eyes.

"Oh, honey." She reached over and took my gloved hand in her own. The room was dimly lit with a small table lamp burning on the table next to her. The shadows made her eyes appear sunken. "You have nothing to apologize for. Really, it's me who should be apologizing."

I stared at her, not comprehending.

"I didn't appreciate how traumatic your mother leaving would be for you and your brother. I thought if I was here to help your dad raise you kids, you would be fine. I thought I could replace your mother. I did my best, but..." She took a deep, shaky breath.

I scooted next to her and wrapped an arm around her bony shoulders. *She's getting so frail,* I thought. "And you did a great job, Mimi. You and Dad both did. Kieran and I would be in much worse shape if it weren't for you." I paused, debating the wisdom of asking my next question. *Oh, what the hell.* "What did Edison Faust do?"

Mimi ran her bony, spotted hands over the pages of the scrapbook, then flipped to a page that contained only one photograph: my mother's high school portrait. "Wasn't she beautiful?" Mimi murmured.

Danielle Lownsdale, Minneapolis Southwest High School class of 1979, was indeed very beautiful. She sat at an angle to the camera, her chin over one shoulder and her big eyes – Kieran's eyes, but hazel – trained on some distant thing. Her lips – *my* lips – formed a small, playful smile. During a time when straight hair and a center part ruled, my mother's tight curls would not be tamed. I could relate. So instead she embraced them, rocking full bangs and a fringe cut. A simple black sweater and a small diamond pendant at her throat completed the senior portrait look.

"She married your dad about a year after this photo was taken." Mimi caressed the photo. "She was already pregnant with Kieran. You came along a little more than a year after he did." She paused, thinking. "You know, some parents wouldn't let their daughter get married and have babies so young. But it never bothered me. Seemed natural, even. I mean, I married your grandfather just before my nineteenth birthday. And my mother wasn't quite twenty when she finally married."

I wondered where she was going with this.

"For us Ainsley women, getting married young has been a way of protecting ourselves. A husband is another barrier the Fausts have to get through to get to us." She glanced at me. "I worry about you, Rae. You're more vulnerable without a husband."

I'm fine, I have a Faust for a boyfriend. "I know, Mimi. But I'm doing okay."

Mimi was silent for a moment. Then: "But sometimes even a husband isn't enough to protect us."

My eyebrows went up.

Mimi turned pages in the scrapbook until she found what she was looking for: a slightly yellowed photo of my mother. She looked earnestly into the camera, her curls, longer now, were mussed. Her eyes were puffy, and her neck was covered with dark, ugly blotches. Mimi took a deep breath. "Your father was always very diligent and usually didn't let your mother go anywhere without him. But he was out of town on a business trip and she needed groceries. She called me up and asked me to go with her to the Red Owl. We figured we wouldn't be out long and there was safety in numbers. So we picked up a few things, then went straight back to the car. Dani loaded the bags into the trunk while I helped you kids into the backseat. Out of nowhere this big blue car pulled up next to Dani, and Edison got out and grabbed her." Mimi paused. "Oh, her screams. They haunt me still, to this day."

I frowned. "When did this happen?" I wracked my brain in search of a memory and came up with nothing.

"August of nineteen eighty-nine."

Just two weeks before Mom left us. I was seven years old. "What did you do?"

"I told you kids to stay put and ran to her as fast as I could. Edison was trying to force her into his car, but he underestimated her strength. She fought him with everything she had. I grabbed one of her arms and pulled. He somehow managed to get his elbow around her neck and looked me dead in the eye as he squeezed. Dani's head turned red and her legs started to kick and she made this awful choking sound. Edison said, 'Let go, Emily, or she will die.'"

I didn't dare blink. "Oh my god. What did you do?"

"I did what any mother would do in my place. I said, 'If she dies, her touch goes with her. Either way you lose, Edison.' And then I kicked him in the crotch as hard as I could with my pointed-toe pump."

I gasped. "Holy shit, Mimi!"

"He let go of Dani and they both went down." Mimi wiped tears from her eyes. "Dani was semi-conscious and breathing, thank goodness. I had to slap her awake and drag her to the car while Edison rolled around on the asphalt and shrieked like a little girl." Was that the ghost of a smile playing around her wrinkled mouth? "We got out of there as fast as we could."

"And this photo was taken after that?"

"Yes. I thought it would be helpful to document her injuries, just in case."

I gazed at my mother's eyes; they were full of utter terror and deep exhaustion. She'd always had to fight so hard just to stay alive, and I realized that by the time Mimi snapped this photo, she had already made her decision.

"It was Mom who decided to leave, wasn't it?" I asked. "You just helped her do it."

Mimi nodded. "I encouraged her to consider separating from her family for everyone's safety, but yes, the choice was hers alone. The close call with Edison, right in front of her children, was the last straw. You and Kieran watched the whole thing happen through the back window of the car." Tears welled in her eyes again. "You both had terrible nightmares for weeks afterward. It was very traumatic for everyone."

"And she wanted to spare us any more trauma," I murmured and touched the photo. "She really was forced to make an impossible decision."

"There's something else."

I looked at Mimi, brows knitted. "Okay."

"Have you ever wondered why Edison is so laser-focused on your mother and doesn't try nearly as hard to take you or me?"

"Well, you've always said he lets us live because we're the only links left to Mom. Although he *has* tried to hurt us." I thought of Nicholas with his syringe full of an untraceable paralytic drug, and Mimi's close call with Morgan and his big black SUV in the supermarket parking lot just the other day.

Mimi nodded. "Yes, that's true. I believe those incidents are Edison lashing out at us when he's frustrated that he can't access Danielle. But he never tries to exploit our touch."

"Because he needs Mom's touch to see the future, instead of the past. That's what you told me ages ago."

"I know. But it's a bit more complicated than that." Mimi lifted her chin and gazed at the darkness outside the family room window. "Our touch *could* be helpful…if he had the right object."

I realized she was right. Mimi's and my ability to interpret psychic energy was bound by the time and space of the object we touched; we could only see what happened directly to or near it, from its perspective. Nicholas had mentioned that Edison was researching gold prices; it stood to reason that he might be hatching a plan to steal someone's stash. Our touch would only be useful to him if he had an object that was present when that person hid or accessed that stash.

"Your mother's touch, on the other hand, is much more advanced. Thanks to Edison." A mirthless chuckle escaped her. "The mercury he poisoned me with significantly altered Danielle's touch. All she needs is something that carries a person's psychic energy. Then her brain is able to find and follow that person's energy in the atmosphere and interpret it as visions."

"Like a dog's nose," I murmured

"Yes. Very much like that. This gives her the ability to see everything that happens to that person throughout his or her life – past, present *and* future."

I stared at Mimi, thunderstruck. She had just destroyed everything I thought I knew about my mother's psychic ability. "So her touch doesn't work like yours and mine, but just shows future events?"

She shook her head.

"Why would you lie to Kieran and me like that?" I asked, more sad than angry. *More secrets, more lies.*

"Everything I've ever done has been for the express purpose of protecting your mother," Mimi said, sounding as tired as I felt.

"You didn't trust us," I said, echoing the bitter words Kieran had spoken over dinner.

"The fewer people who know, the safer your mother is." There was no contrition in her voice. "I don't know how, but it seems that Edison has an inkling of your mother's power. That's why he wants her so badly and has no time for you or me."

I leaned back into the couch and rubbed my face. "Holy shit," I sighed. *This changes everything,* I thought. Suddenly bringing Mom home seemed like a terrible idea.

"I hope you can forgive us, Rae." Mimi's voice trembled.

I ran an arm behind Mimi's bony shoulders and pulled her in for a side hug. My temple touched hers. She smelled like baby powder. "Of course I forgive you, Mimi. Kieran does, too. We know you've done the best you could under the circumstances." I kissed her soft, wrinkled cheek. "I love you."

"I love you too, doll." She pulled back and placed a warm gloved hand on my cheek. "Now off to bed with you."

I didn't argue.

Tuesday, July 13, 2021

CHAPTER 9

For once I awoke refreshed, able to get some real sleep without the effects of alcohol. Not enough sleep because I was up so late with Mimi, but I would take what I could get. I walked into the River Junction Police Department promptly at eight o'clock freshly groomed and holding a mostly-empty cup of coffee.

"Hello, Ms. O'Rourke." Officer Solomon was back at her front desk post. She slid something that at first appeared to be a credit card through the hole in the fiberglass partition. It had my name printed on it. "Here's your badge. Wear this on you anytime you're here at the station, and just scan it to open any door."

"Thanks," I said, and then held the card up to the black scanner set in the wall between Solomon's window and the door to the back office. I heard a click and pulled on the handle; the door popped right open. "Sweet," I said and gave Solomon a big smile. "I've got the power now!" I said this jokingly, but was actually serious; I really did feel powerful with a radio-frequency key to the RJPD.

Solomon laughed. "Do you know where you're going?"

"Yes ma'am." I waved and headed down the hall toward our war room. Hendricks had arrived just moments before me and was setting a cardboard carrier holding two large premium coffees on the desk. He had left the patrol uniform at home today, opting instead for a white button-down shirt, the sleeves rolled up to his elbows and tucked into a pair of pressed khaki pants. I wished him a good morning.

"Good morning!" His big smile made my insides tingle. "I, uh, I didn't know what you liked for your coffee, so I just got us both dark roast, black."

"Exactly the way I like it." I tossed my gas station coffee cup in the garbage can and picked up one of Hendricks' coffees. It smelled like heaven and tasted like happiness in a cup. "Thank you."

"Everything all right at home?"

"Yes, thanks. Everyone was where they were supposed to be when I got there."

"I'm glad to hear it," he said. "How's your dad?"

"He'll pull through." I gave Hendricks an ironic smile. "He has a big black bruise on his forehead, but the cut is scabbed over. He should be good as new in a couple weeks."

Hendricks's intense green eyes held mine. "Good. So what's on our agenda today?"

Was it getting hot in here, or was it just me? "James Locke," I said. "Mia's neighbor. I think he's gotta be our first stop. And we have to get our hands on Mia's text messages."

"I talked to Sergeant Rooney after you left yesterday. He told me to work with Julia Gomez, the city attorney, to get a subpoena. Should be ready today, and then off to the phone company it goes."

"How long will that take?"

Hendricks shrugged. "A few days, probably. I think we'll have plenty to keep us busy in the meantime."

I held up my coffee. "Let's go."

Hendricks obtained the keys to an unmarked RJPD car and we climbed in. "Ugh," I said as I set my purse on the passenger side floor between my feet. "It smells like stale french fries in here."

Hendricks used buttons set in the driver's side door to roll all of the windows down. "Sorry about that," he said. "Cops tend to live on a fast food diet. Detective Phelps last had this car, and he is particularly fond of the double cheeseburger meal."

"So I see." I picked a petrified french fry out of the cupholder to make room for my coffee.

Hendricks steered the car out of the back parking lot and headed west on Greenhaven Road, past neat little postwar homes with tidy lawns and some of the prettiest flower gardens I'd ever seen. There was a pride of ownership here in River Junction that seemed to be lacking elsewhere, even in my dad's upper-middle-class south Minneapolis neighborhood. I said something to that effect as Hendricks waited for the light at Fourth Street before making a right turn.

"Yeah. People are proud to live here. River Junction is a unique place, in the sense that once families settle here, they tend to stay. It's the small town that has everything you need, and it's an easy drive to Minneapolis for everything you want. There's no reason to leave." He glanced at me. "Well, maybe there's one reason to leave."

I knew what he meant. "Mimi – that's my grandmother – sometimes says that she considers River Junction to be her home, even though she's never actually lived here. If it weren't for that old psychopath, all of the Ainsleys would probably still be here." I paused, then sighed. "Everything would have been different for us." A weight settled over my heart at the thought: *We would have had normal lives.* The idea was so foreign, yet so alluring...like a mysterious and devastatingly beautiful woman.

"Just another ordinary family," Hendricks said, as if he were reading my mind.

"Right." I stared out the window, not really seeing the houses and perfect landscapes whizz by. Hendricks left me alone with my thoughts of my parents, my Mimi, and the unintended consequences of impossible choices – until we pulled up in front of a meticulously maintained 1920s Craftsman bungalow. James Locke's house was in an older neighborhood south of downtown River Junction, a couple blocks from the Bourbon River. Just across the street stood a very old two-story Federal-style house with narrow windows and a mansard roof set far back on an oversized lot. The brick had been painted white, the trim and shutters were a dark green, and it was all peeling and chipping. I guessed it had been built before the turn of the twentieth century, and it was likely the original farmhouse in this neighborhood. It even still had its carriage house, long ago converted into living quarters. Probably rental. *I bet that's where Mia lived,* I thought.

Hendricks and I got out of the car and followed the concrete walkway that led from the curb to Locke's front door. I let Hendricks lead, since he was the one with the badge. He knocked on the door and then stepped back.

The door opened and an elderly bald man who quite literally looked like an owl peered at us with huge hazel eyes. His face was wide and jowly, mostly gray hair grew gaily from his ears, and his tiny nose pointed down at the tip. I couldn't stop my mouth from falling open, but I blinked and quickly recovered.

"Mr. Locke?" Hendricks gave the old man a friendly smile.

"Yes?" The look on Locke's face was decidedly less friendly. Not what I expected in a town that bills itself "The Friendliest City in America." But then again Edison Faust, the living antithesis of anything friendly, *did* live here.

Hendricks held up his badge. "My name is Jesse Hendricks, I'm with the River Junction Police Department." He gestured toward me. "This is Ms. O'Rourke."

"What can I do for you?" Locke eyed my gloved hands suspiciously. I noticed a framed photograph of two fluffy Pomeranian dogs on the wall behind him.

"We'd like to ask you a few questions about Mia Masterson."

Locke blinked, surprised, and all suspicion fell out of his face. "Oh, my goodness." He stepped outside and pulled the door closed behind him. "It's been a long time since I heard that name."

"Did you know her?" I asked.

"She lived just over there." He pointed at the carriage house. *I knew it,* I thought. "Sweet girl. She would sometimes watch my dogs while Joyce and I went to see her sister down in Owatonna." He shook his head sadly. "I'm the only one left now. Joyce passed about a year after Mia went missing. Cancer."

"I'm very sorry," Hendricks said as he pulled a small notebook from his pants pocket, ready to get down to business. "Mr. Locke, we were wondering –"

He was trying to carry on like a lonely old man hadn't just dropped an emotional bomb on us. I interrupted him, sensing that Locke wanted to talk more. "Are those your dogs on the wall in there, Mr. Locke?"

He gave me a grateful look. He was glad just to have someone to talk to, and happy to talk about his canine companions. "Yep. Minerva and Athena. They were sisters from the same litter. They had two brothers too, they were named Poseidon and Triton."

I smiled. "I get it. The Greek and Roman names of the same gods."

Locke nodded vigorously. "Their parents were Zeus and Juno. Anyway, Minerva, she never adjusted to Joyce being gone. She just stopped eating and passed within a few weeks. Athena was such a wonderful companion. She kept me company until her kidneys failed last year." He pointed to a large sugar maple tree in his yard. "They're both buried under that tree. The leaves turn bright red every fall."

I wanted to ask him if Joyce was buried under there too, but decided it wasn't a very funny joke. "I'm very sorry for your loss," I said, meaning every word. I knew how it felt to lose a loved one.

"Yeah, me too." Hendricks kept his eyes on his shoes. He too was familiar with the feeling. I recalled my vision of a sheriff's deputy delivering bad news and wondered who he'd lost.

"I appreciate you two listening to an old man go on about his dogs," Locke said. "What can I tell you about Mia?"

Hendricks flipped through his notebook until he found a clean page. "I understand you saw her the morning she went missing."

Locke pointed a few feet down the walk. "I was standing right there, watering the petunias. Joyce was fond of petunias, said all the different colors reminded her of a rainbow. I took them out after she passed. It was just too hard to see them." Sadness blanketed his eyes again, then he blinked and refocused on Hendricks. "I always gave them a drink first thing in the morning after my coffee, so it was pretty early."

"Detective Baker's report said you saw her putting baby Isabel into her car around seven forty-five."

"That sounds about right."

"And that she was wearing black yoga pants and a white cropped shirt." Another nod. "Did she see you or talk to you?"

Locke shook his head. "I tried to wave, but she didn't pay me any attention. She was moving pretty slow."

I frowned and tilted my head. "What do you mean?"

"She was kinda hunched over at the waist, like her stomach hurt. Taking slow steps. She seemed to have a hard time carrying the carseat too. Stopped once between the front door and her car to set it down and rest."

I turned to look at the carriage house across the street. It was a cute little story-and-a-half structure with a dormer window and a single car garage, clad in wood shakes painted white like the house. If she parked her car in front of the garage, the walk to the front door would have been roughly twenty feet. I looked back at Hendricks. "That's not a very long walk. And the carseat couldn't have weighed more than fifteen pounds, including the baby."

"Well, Mia was only four days postpartum," Hendricks pointed out. "And just got home from the hospital the day before."

He made a good point. I couldn't imagine any woman's body being okay for a long time after birthing an entire baby. *I bet*

77

everything hurt, I thought. I stared at the carriage house and contemplated that while Hendricks asked Locke another question.

"Do you know where she was going?"

Locke lifted his thin arm and pointed to his right. "All I saw was she started the car and drove off that way."

"South," Hendricks muttered as he noted this.

Movement at the big house caught my eye. A middle-aged man with black hair stood outside the front door, watching us. He wore an oversized gray t-shirt with IN MY DEFENSE I WAS LEFT UNSUPERVISED printed on it and a pair of black basketball shorts. "Who's that?" I asked Locke.

He scoffed. "That's Alex Blackett. A bigger idiot never lived, except maybe his father."

We thanked Locke for his time, and Hendricks gave him a business card. "If you think of anything else, give me a call. No matter how small or trivial."

Locke waved as we crossed the street toward Alex Blackett and his big old house. He met us on the sidewalk and shook Hendricks' hand. His distended belly suggested a great affinity for beer, and his hair, still more pepper than salt, was overdue for a trim.

"How can I help you, man?" Blackett asked Hendricks.

"We'd like to ask you a few questions about Mia Masterson," Hendricks said.

"She lived in your carriage house, didn't she?" I asked.

Blackett slowly shifted his brown eyes to my face, then back to Hendricks before saying, "Yeah, she rented my carriage house for a few years."

Hendricks and I exchanged a brief glance; it seemed we both thought it a bit odd that Blackett so pointedly addressed Hendricks and not me. A mild perma-frown settled over my forehead.

"Were you home the day she went missing?" Hendricks asked.

"Yeah, I was home. But I didn't see her. I was sleeping. I work overnights at the hospital."

What time did you get home that morning?"

"My shift ends at six-thirty. I'm usually home and asleep by seven o'clock."

"You're up now," I pointed out.

Blackett didn't even acknowledge me. "Day off," he told Hendricks.

"Do you have any trouble getting to sleep in the mornings?" Hendricks asked.

Blackett shook his head. "Nah, not anymore. I have blackout curtains on my windows–" he pointed to two of the windows on the second floor "–so my room stays nice and dark."

I decided I wasn't going to let this jerk exclude me from the conversation. "Alex, you reported Mia missing on September twenty-fifth. Why did it take you three days to notice she was gone?"

The eyes slid back to me, and the contempt in them was clear. "Did you hear me just say I work overnights at the hospital? Or are you deaf?"

Hendricks opened his mouth, but I spoke before he could get a word out. "Excuse me, what is your problem?"

Blackett crossed his arms over his chest, resting them on his belly. "You ain't a cop. I don't have to talk to you."

What a prick. "Listen here, you –"

Hendricks laid a hand on my shoulder, ending my tirade before it started. Which was probably a good thing; Blackett's behavior was so appalling that it was highly likely I would say something I might regret later. "Look, Alex, Ms. O'Rourke is a consultant with the police department and has full authority to work with me to investigate Mia Masterson's disappearance. Please show her some respect."

Blackett gave me a long, measured look, then shrugged. "Mia was a server at two bars, and I worked overnights at the hospital. We just didn't see each other that much. I didn't know she wasn't home until I realized I didn't see her car for a couple of days."

"What did she drive?" Hendricks asked, as if we didn't already know.

"Jeep Liberty. Black. Two thousand four, I think."

"What did you do then?" I had calmed down enough to reengage in the conversation.

"I knocked on her door, and when she didn't answer I let myself in. She wasn't there, and the baby wasn't either."

"Did the place look like there had been any kind of a struggle?" Hendricks asked.

Blackett shook his head. "Nope. Looked just like it normally did, with baby stuff everywhere. It looked to me like wherever she went, she meant to come right back."

Hendricks wrote something in his notebook.

"So you called the police?" I asked.

"I called her bosses first. Just to see if she went back to work, even though the baby was only a few days old. I could see Mia doing that. And I'm sure she needed money."

"What were her bosses' names?" Hendricks was still jotting notes.

"Uh, well, Cody Brock owned the Majestic back then."

"Shit," Hendricks muttered as he wrote.

"What? What's the deal with Cody Brock?" I asked.

"He died in a car accident five years ago," Hendricks said, looking up from his notebook. "You might have heard about it in Minneapolis too. He was stopped on the Bridge Street bridge for traffic that was stacked up behind the red light at Greenhaven Road, and a semi rear-ended his car at highway speed."

I winced.

"The truck flipped Cody's Mini Cooper over the side of the bridge like a quarter and it ended up upside down in the Mississippi River," Blackett said.

I snapped my fingers. "I do remember that," I said. Nelson Swain, traffic reporter at the Minneapolis Daily News & Review at the time, wrote those stories. Both drivers were killed in the crash: Cody Brock's death had been ruled an accident with multiple causes: blunt force trauma to the head and chest, with drowning as a contributing factor. Gordon Munson, the semi driver, had suffered an aneurysm and was probably dead before his truck hit Cody's car. Six other people were injured. "It was really tragic."

Hendricks nodded. "It was. A real shock to the community, that's for sure. A guy from Minneapolis named David Forrester bought the Majestic Saloon at auction a few months after Cody died, and he still owns it now."

That was a name I recognized. David Forrester presided over a Twin Cities nightlife empire, with a nightclub and three bars in

Minneapolis, two bars in St. Paul, and six more bar and grills in surrounding communities – including River Junction. He was a frequent subject in the pages of the Daily News & Review, although I, as crime reporter, never wrote about him. That meant he'd managed to keep his nose pretty clean.

"Who was Mia's other boss?" I asked.

"Tom McCarthy, and he still owns the Rummery," Blackett said. "Tom and Cody didn't see Mia since before the baby was born either. That's when I called the police and put in a missing person's report."

I had an idea. "What did you end up doing with all of her stuff, Alex?"

He shrugged. "I had most of it hauled away. I kept a few things I thought her dad might want, but he never came to pick them up. I think the box is still in my garage."

"We would like to see that box," Hendricks said. I looked at him and knew he was thinking the same thing I was: Mia's possessions might hold clues only my touch could unearth.

Blackett shrugged and shambled toward his garage, beer belly leading the way. I stepped up next to Hendricks and said in a low voice, "Ninety-five percent of the information we've gotten so far today is not in Mia's case file."

Hendricks bobbed his head wordlessly, his eyes on Blackett's back.

"Poor Mia," I said softly.

Blackett returned holding a slightly yellowed box with a lid. He pushed the box against my chest. "Here. Take it."

Apparently he and I had not resolved our differences – whatever they were – but for Hendricks' sake I kept my mouth shut and took the box.

Hendricks gave Blackett a tired look. "Really?"

Blackett shrugged and showed Hendricks a mouth full of crooked, yellowing teeth. "Can't help it. She reminds me too much of my second ex-wife. That mouthy bitch didn't know her place either."

I'd had enough. "I'll see you in the car," I said to Hendricks, then turned and made my way back across the street.

James Locke was still in front of his house, sweeping his walk and keeping a close eye on us. He waved at me. "Did you get what you need?" he called.

"Yes, thank you." I pulled the rear passenger door open and set Mia's box on the backseat. Then I climbed into the front seat and glared at Alex Blackett through the window, my arms crossed over my chest. *Asshole.*

Hendricks shook Blackett's hand and came back to the car. He grinned when he saw me pouting in the front seat. "Oh, don't let that creep get to you, Raegan."

"I can see why he has multiple ex-wives," I muttered. "Jackass."

"I got Mia's father's name and number from him too," Hendricks said. "The number he had back in twenty-ten, anyway. We'll need to try and get a hold of him."

"I want to look through that box." I was jazzed to have my first chance to use my touch on this case.

"Let's do it," Hendricks said, pulling away from the curb and leaving James Locke in the rearview, still holding his broom.

CHAPTER 10

Back at the station, a cacophony of voices and ringing phones – familiar sounds that I strongly associated with the newsroom at the Daily News & Review – drifted through the open door to our office as Hendricks set the box on the desk and removed the lid. The strong musty odor of years of neglect made my eyes water.

The box's contents were depressingly sparse: a small framed photo of Mia and an older man I thought might be her father, standing next to the cab of a semi truck; a rusty cast iron figurine of a horse reared up on its hind legs; a stack of wrinkled, water-damaged papers; a yellowed teddy bear, its fur matted and one eye missing; a hospital card with tiny footprints no longer than my pinky finger inked on it; and various odds and ends. I had to admit that Alex Blackett appeared to have done a good job of at least trying to save things that were important. *Maybe there's a heart buried somewhere in that beer-soaked body after all,* I thought.

"Where do you want to start?" Hendricks asked.

"The horse," I said, taking off my gloves. "Would you mind taking it out of the box for me?"

He did, and set it on the desk in front of us. It was black, about eight inches tall, and looked heavy.

"Any particular reason why the horse and not, say, the teddy bear?" Hendricks asked. His bright green eyes roved over everything as if he didn't want to miss a single detail.

"Because hard materials trap and retain psychic energy better than soft materials. So the horse is going to show me a lot more than the teddy bear would. Especially because the horse is made of metal."

Hendricks nodded slowly as he absorbed this information. "So what's going to happen? How does this work?"

I blinked, realizing that this would be the first time I'd ever intentionally used my touch in front of someone other than my family. I suddenly felt awkward and vulnerable, like I was about to spill my deepest darkest secret during a game of Truth or Dare, and my heart skipped a beat. "Oh. Um, well, I'm going to put my bare fingers on the horse, and everything after that happens in my head. To you I'll probably look like I'm sleeping or staring blankly at the wall."

Hendricks abruptly stood, and for a split second I thought he was going to leave the room. *Too weird for him,* I thought, and my stomach fell. Instead he closed the door. "There," he said as he sat back down. "Nobody needs to walk by and ask questions we don't want to answer. None of their business, right?"

The sweet gesture made me smile. "Thanks, Jesse."

"No problem." He smiled back and gestured at the horse. "Please, carry on."

I took a deep breath and said "Okay," more to myself than to Hendricks. Then I laid my bare fingertips on the rough, corroded surface of the old figurine and closed my eyes. All thoughts of Hendricks vanished, and visions like old-timey film reels bloomed behind my eyelids. I watched a younger, thinner, and less grizzled Alex Blackett place Mia Masterson's most important possessions, including the old cast iron horse, inside the box and replace the lid. All I could see after that was pitch black, and then the vision faded and floated away like the last ash from a dying campfire.

It was replaced by older, even more faded visions from before Mia went missing. I could tell that the horse figurine had been situated in a corner of the small, well-worn living room of Mia's rental carriage house, and for the longest time I watched the mundanity of an ordinary woman's ordinary life.

Here she was, walking in from the kitchen holding a steaming cup of tea in her hand, hair wet, her bathrobe barely able to cover her pregnant belly.

Here she was again, running past the door to the kitchen with a hand over her mouth. She looked a bit green in the gills, and I wondered if she was suffering from morning sickness.

And there she was, walking in the front door after a late night at one of her server jobs and collapsing on the couch. She had no visible baby bump, but exhaustion carved deep lines under her eyes.

Gradually the visions of those mundane events grayed out and fluttered away too, and the next one began. It was a doozy.

∞

Mia sat on a worn old overstuffed chair, her feet tucked underneath her, staring pensively out the front window. She seemed to be waiting for someone. Her dark pixie cut hair was carefully mussed, and she was casually dressed in a pair of low-waisted boot cut jeans, a black belt covered in silver studs, and a sleeveless white crop top. Giant silver hoops dangled from her earlobes, and her delicate face was expertly made up. She clearly was not pregnant. Not yet, anyway.

She jumped up from the chair and anxiously paced the room. At one point she stopped right in front of me; I could have reached out and touched her breasts, if I were able. She stood on tiptoe and reached up. Adjusting something on a shelf above me, maybe? She wore a silver necklace I hadn't noticed before. Its pendant, shaped like a fiery sun, rested just below her collarbones.

Suddenly she stopped what she was doing and turned to the front door. Whoever she was waiting for had arrived.

She went to the door and threw it open. A man stepped over the threshold. He was not much taller than Mia, at least ten years older than she was, and handsome in an unconventional, basset hound sort of way. She closed the door behind him and they made their way across the living room, talking animatedly and laughing as if they were old friends who had a lot of catching up to do. The man carried a sheaf of papers; as he set them on the coffee table I caught a glimpse of RUMMERY BAR & GRILL *printed on the top sheet.*

This must be Tom Mc–

The pair stopped in front of the couch and embraced so passionately that my thought cut cleanly off and my face and neck suddenly felt hot. This wasn't the first time I'd encountered people having sex in a vision; in fact, it happened so often that I'd never felt compelled to use my real eyes to watch porn. I was continually amazed at the variety of places people chose to do the horizontal – or vertical – mambo: in an elevator, in a rental car, in a movie theater, and, incredibly, in a portable toilet. No place was sacred, and I always felt like a complete peeper even though I knew it was only happening in my head.

Mia wrapped her arms around the man's neck and pulled him down to the couch. They lay like that, the man on top of her, and fooled around for quite some time. Arms waved, legs stretched, hands clenched, and tongues flicked. Clothing came off gradually; Mia's crop top went first and landed in the middle of the living room floor. The man's golf shirt was next, crumpled in a heap atop the papers on the coffee table. Eventually all that remained were his black boxer briefs and her lacy white bra and matching panties. They stopped in the middle of the action and exchanged a few words while still nose-to-nose. The man lifted himself off of Mia and stood up, his engorged penis standing at attention. He had a pretty nice body for a man approaching forty; his abs and chest were still relatively toned, but a slight layer of fat suggested the beginnings of a classic dad bod. Easy access to beer and bar food did that to a guy, I supposed.

Mia scrambled off the couch. Her hair stood in crazy clumps. She took the man's hand and led him into the kitchen, ostensibly headed toward the stairs that led to the bedroom on the second floor.

They disappeared from view, and the vision faded to black.

∞

I lifted my fingers from the figurine and opened my eyes. Hendricks still sat next to me, his eyes trained on my face. "Welcome back," he said.

"Thanks." I put my gloves back on.

You were gone for like ten minutes," Hendricks said. "I was beginning to wonder if I should try to wake you."

I smiled, touched by his concern and also glad he didn't try to wake me. I didn't know what would have happened. Mimi was my constant guide when it came to my touch, but she'd never talked about that. Nobody was supposed to know about my touch.

"What did you see?" Hendricks asked.

I took a deep breath. "Mia was sleeping with a guy I'm pretty sure was her boss."

"Really," Hendricks breathed. "Which one?"

"It must have been Tom McCarthy," I said. "He was holding some papers and I saw the words 'Rummery Bar and Grill' printed on them."

Hendricks' eyes sparkled. "Is that why your whole head turned red all of a sudden? Did you see aaalllll the action?" He playfully leaned a shoulder into me.

Heat crawled up my neck. "Stop," I said, and smacked his arm.

His eyes held mine for about half a second longer than was necessary. My heart jackrabbited in my chest, and I shifted my gaze back to my hands. *Nicholas,* I thought, in a futile effort to calm my guilty conscience. *Nicholas.*

Hendricks chuckled and moved his chair away from me. "I guess a conversation with Tom McCarthy is in order."

"We should get a hold of Mia's father too," I said. My voice didn't tremble, much to my relief.

Hendricks scooted his chair around to the other side of the desk, pulling his notebook out of his pants pocket as he went. He picked up the phone and dialed the number Alex Blackett had given him.

"Hello. I'm looking for Mike Masterson, please." Hendricks paused for a moment, listening, then said, "My name is Jesse Hendricks, I'm calling from the police department in River Junction, Minnesota. I'd like to ask him a few —" Another pause. "Oh. Oh no, I'm very sorry to hear that. When?" He tossed me a glance that told me we'd just hit a dead end. Literally and figuratively. I exhaled heavily, feeling a bit deflated. "Were you married long?" Hendricks made a note. "Did he ever mention his daughter Mia?" Another nod, another note. "All right. Thank you, Mrs. Masterson. Please accept my condolences for your loss. You're welcome. Goodbye."

He placed the handset back in its cradle and looked at me frankly. "He drove his semi rig off a bridge outside Gila Bend, Arizona six months ago. His widow, they'd only been married five years when he died, says she knew about Mia, but he rarely spoke of her. It was too painful. She said his death was ruled an accident, but she wouldn't be surprised if he'd intentionally crashed. His heart was broken."

I thought about how frantic and terrified I'd been when my own dad was missing for two hours. I couldn't imagine what it did to a man, wondering where his daughter was for over ten years. "Poor guy."

Hendricks sighed. "Maybe that's why he never picked Mia's stuff up from Alex. He just couldn't handle it."

The thought of a grieving father abandoning his daughter's possessions was so tragic, tears effervesced behind my eyes. I breathed deep and blinked. "Do you think he knew he was a grandfather?"

"His wife said he was making plans to come back to Minnesota to visit Mia and meet baby Isabel when they went missing."

"God, that makes this whole thing even more tragic than it already was," I said.

"Yeah."

We sat in friendly silence for a moment, and then my phone chirped. I glanced at it; Todd Waterman's name flashed on the screen. Todd was the editor of the Minneapolis Daily News & Review, and my boss until two days ago. I frowned and debated declining the call.

"Do you need to take that?" Hendricks asked.

I sighed. "No, but I will anyway." I swiped to answer the call and said, "Hey Todd."

"Raegan!" No hello, no preamble, no small talk. "I have a huge story for you."

I rolled my eyes. "I don't work for you anymore, remember? Or did you not get the memo?"

"Yeah, but this is a big one. A big *cold* one. There's nobody else I would trust with it. Come on, at least hear me out."

Damn it, I thought. *He gets me.* "All right, I'll hear you out. Let me call you back from the car."

"Cool," Waterman said, and was gone.

I looked at Hendricks. "I should probably go."

He smiled. "Go. We'll track Tom McCarthy down in the morning. I mean, after some coffee, if you're up for it." His face turned pink.

I blinked, confused. Coffee came before everything. "Yes, I usually bring coffee with me."

"No, I mean, maybe we could meet up for coffee before we talk to McCarthy." His blush intensified, and his eyes didn't quite meet mine.

It finally clicked, and my heart quickened. "Oh!" A nervous laugh fell from my mouth. "I'm sorry, I –"

Hendricks chuckled too, and the tension was broken. "No, I'm sorry. I'm a doof. I didn't mean to make things awkward, I just thought we could grab coffee first thing in the morning."

"We can. Absolutely. Where?"

Uh, well, there's a little coffee shop on Bridge Street, called Beananza. They're world famous for their cold brew."

"I'm sold," I said, and stood to gather my belongings. "What time?"

"Eight o'clock?"

"See you then." I gave Hendricks a little wave and made my way back to my car.

I had a guy to call about another cold case.

CHAPTER 11

"This is Todd." Waterman's voice filled the interior of my SUV as I navigated through downtown River Junction.

"Todd, when someone resigns their position, that means they don't have to take your calls anymore."

"Then why did you answer?" Waterman sounded more amused than apologetic.

I sighed. "Because you usually have something interesting brewing. And old habits also die hard."

He chuckled. "I think it means you miss me," he said. "You can come back, you know. Anytime. No questions asked."

This was interesting coming from a man who, until I solved a twenty-five-year-old cold case and brought him an exclusive story, was convinced I'd gotten information for my stories by sleeping around. Now he was tripping over himself to lay out the red carpet for me in an effort to get me back into his newsroom. I'd never trusted him, and still didn't.

The real reason I'd called him back? Icebox Investigations. I wanted to hear about this story he had. *Could be a lead for my next job,* I thought. *After I find Mia.*

"Tell me what you've got," I said. I left historic downtown River Junction and headed south on the highway, slipping my sunglasses onto my face. Strip malls, banks, and chain restaurants whizzed by on either side of me.

I heard the pages of a notebook flipping on Todd's end of the line. "Have you ever heard of...." A pause while he scanned his notes. "Angel Baby?"

I frowned. "I don't know, maybe?"

"We were inspired by your Catclaw Kids story and spent most of this morning's editorial meeting discussing other cold cases we might want to take a look at. Tucker Renny mentioned the Angel Baby case, said he almost lost his job over it."

I needed more. "Details?" I prompted.

"A guy fishing for bullheads in the Mississippi River found the body of a baby girl caught up in some fallen trees along the shoreline."

"In Minneapolis?"

"Yeah." Waterman turned a couple pages. "By the Camden Bridge. North side of town."

"When?"

"Back in twenty-ten," Waterman said. "Renny said the case had huge coverage at first, front page for weeks, and police even had a potential suspect. But nothing panned out and the case went cold."

All of this tugged at something deep in my brain, but I couldn't quite catch it. In 2010 I was a general assignment reporter for the Daily News & Review, and didn't recall working on this story. I would have remembered it if I had, I was sure. "That's very sad, but what does it have to do with me?"

"It's a cold case," Waterman said. "Those are your specialty. The Catclaw Kids has been a huge story since we broke it. I would love for you to do it again. For me."

I sighed. "Todd, I'm working on a case. I don't really have the capacity to take on another one right now."

Waterman asked about that, and I gave him a quick rundown of Mia Masterson's disappearance.

"When you solve it, write a story. I'll buy it from you."

This was a new twist I hadn't considered for my fledgling detective agency. Use my touch to solve cold cases and then write and sell news stories about them? It was the ideal situation. "A buck a word, and you've got a deal."

Waterman exhaled air directly into his phone, filling the inside of my car with a tornado's roar. "You drive a hard bargain, O'Rourke. Fine, it's a deal. But don't you be coming to me with a five-thousand-word fluff piece, understood?"

I chuckled. "Renny's the wordy one, not me."

"Renny is the reason we have proofreaders and editors," Waterman said. "Listen, at least let me send you some stuff on this Angel Baby story. Read up on it. Maybe you'll decide to tackle that one next. As far as I know, it's been sitting at MPD collecting dust since the last chief was fired. I mean, the chief before last. What's her face."

I took a brief moment to mentally pat myself on the back for the dismissals of the last two chiefs of the Minneapolis Police Department. The most recent one colluded with the Hennepin County attorney in an attempt to cover up a rape committed by an MPD patrol officer. I called them out on their lies in the middle of a press conference, and both Chief Brent Henke and County

Attorney James Litchfield were promptly fired after my story hit the paper. With Henke's predecessor a year prior, I was chasing down a lead on a potential embezzlement scheme at a local charity when I stumbled over evidence implicating both the chief and the governor's wife, who was the charity's primary benefactor, in the fraud. Uncovering the steamy affair between them was icing on the cake. My reporting exposed both the fraud and the affair, ending Sonya Hartman's fifteen-year reign as Chief of Police at the Minneapolis Police Department.

I turned my attention back to Todd Waterman on the phone and conceded. "Fine. Send me what you've got. But it's going to get none of my attention until I find Mia Masterson."

"Fair enough. I have no doubt you will find her, Raegan. You found the Catclaw Kids, I'm pretty sure you can find anybody."

I still didn't believe Waterman had any confidence in my investigative chops, so I was strangely touched by his compliment. "Thanks, Todd."

"Watch your email," he said, and ended the call.

∞

My dad's house was empty when I arrived. Mimi had left a note on the kitchen counter: K and I are running errands. Back later. Dad working late. So I cracked open a new bottle of chardonnay and poured myself a glass – one that was not accompanied by disapproving glances from concerned family members. Then I took the glass and my laptop out to the back porch. I settled into the thick cushions of the loveseat, opened my computer, and took a big drink of wine while my email loaded. The chardonnay was cold and tart. I may have even smacked my lips once or twice. I'd been so good the last few days, I deserved a celebratory drink.

I pulled up the email from Todd Waterman and scanned it. He hadn't bothered with a message, simply pasted a few web links into the email. I clicked the first one, which took me to a Minneapolis Daily News & Review article dated September 26, 2010.

Body of infant found in Mississippi River
Baby girl discovered by local fisherman
Tucker Renny, Daily News & Review
Sunday, September 26, 2010

Minneapolis police are investigating after the remains of a newborn girl were found in the Mississippi River just south of the Camden Bridge on Saturday afternoon. A local fisherman called the police at 3:55 p.m. after making the gruesome discovery.

"Our investigators are working with the Medical Examiner's Office to determine the circumstances surrounding this baby's death and how she ended up in the river," said Minneapolis Police Chief Sonya Hartman. "No further information will be released at this time."

Anyone with information should call 911 or file an anonymous tip with CrimeStoppers at 1-800-222-3333.

It was the typical "this happened but we don't know anything yet" story. As usual, more details trickled out in subsequent stories, as Tucker tracked people down and interviewed them. He'd started with the fisherman who found the baby's body.

Infant found in Mississippi River still unidentified
A day of fishing turns traumatic for local man
Tucker Renny, Daily News & Review
Monday, September 27, 2010

Lorenzo Garcia was fishing for bullheads from the dock at the Mississippi River Boat Ramp when his line got caught up in a clump of fallen trees along the shoreline. He walked over to untangle his line, not knowing that his life was about to turn upside down.

"I didn't know what it was," Garcia, 50, of Minneapolis said. "I just saw a little blob in the water, stuck between branches. I thought it was a plastic shopping bag, or maybe some kid lost his sweatshirt."

A couple of pokes with a long branch revealed something else: the body of an infant, clad in sleeper pajamas. Garcia immediately called the police, who arrived within minutes at the public access, just off Washington Avenue North and below 42nd Avenue North on the west side of the river. Authorities secured the scene and recovered the baby's remains.

"Lord, I was so scared," Garcia said. "I knew the baby was dead. She had scrapes all over her head and her face, and holes in her pajamas. The pajamas had a little yellow duck on them. I'll never forget it. So innocent, you know? I'm a father, and I felt so sorry for the little angel baby. I made the sign of the cross and prayed for her little soul."

When asked to corroborate Garcia's description of the infant's condition, Minneapolis Police Chief Sonya Hartman had no comment. "This is an ongoing investigation. We hope an autopsy will help us identify this baby and find out what happened to her. We have no further details to share until then."

Anyone with information should call 911 or file an anonymous tip with CrimeStoppers at 1-800-222-3333.

I couldn't shake the feeling that this story was associated with something important in my life, but my ability to connect the dots remained maddeningly out of reach. I finished my wine and clicked into the next article, hoping to find another clue.

"Angel Baby" ID still elusive
Autopsy offers no new information
Tucker Renny, Daily News & Review
Tuesday, September 28, 2010

Minneapolis police announced Monday that an autopsy on so-called "Angel Baby," the infant whose body was found in the Mississippi River over the weekend, has offered no new information about her identity. The Hennepin County Medical Examiner's Office was able to estimate her age, approximately one week old, and determine her cause of death as drowning.

"This child suffered horrific injuries," Minneapolis Police Chief Sonya Hartman said during a hastily assembled press conference on Monday afternoon. "We don't know her name, and we don't know how she got in the river, or where. But we will find out." She declined to answer further questions.

Anyone with information should call 911 or file an anonymous report with CrimeStoppers at 1-800-222-3333.

Frustrated, I moved to the next article. But not before I poured myself a fresh glass of wine and took a generous sip. My whole body felt warm.

New twist in Angel Baby case
Wisconsin man and infant daughter disappeared in 2009
Tucker Renny, Daily News & Review
Sunday, October 31, 2010

More than a month after the body of an unidentified newborn baby girl, dubbed Angel Baby, was found in the Mississippi River in north Minneapolis, authorities may finally have a lead.

Police confirmed Saturday that they are investigating whether Angel Baby could be ten-day-old Ashley Gibson, who disappeared along with her father Peter from Shawano, Wisconsin on December 27, 2009. Peter's wife Lola reported her husband and daughter missing when they didn't return home from a Christmas gathering with Peter's extended family. There has been no trace of either since then.

"We continue to tirelessly search for Angel Baby's identity and the person who killed her. We are following up on every lead," police said in a statement. "We will release further information as it becomes available."

Anyone with information should call 911 or file an anonymous tip with CrimeStoppers at 1-800-222-3333.

My eyes kept going back to the date on this article; my brain was shrouded in a light wine fog, so it took me a bit to figure it out. It finally hit me: Halloween 2010 was the day after I first met Nicholas. After that the memories started popping up like whack-a-moles.

Angel Baby had tripped something in my brain because it was the biggest local story of 2010, and Tucker, as investigative reporter at the time, was the lucky one assigned to it. When every update from the police started to sound the same (*This is still an active investigation, we don't have a suspect in custody, we do not believe there's a threat to the public*), Tucker leveraged his considerable connections to conduct his own investigation and play it out in the paper. The higher-ups in Minneapolis were not amused.

This brought up another memory: of our editor at the time, Lou Brown, making a point of talking to Sonya Hartman about the Angel Baby story at the masquerade ball. They'd been deep in conversation for the better part of an hour; Lou never said what they talked about, but now I thought I knew. Hartman tried to talk Lou out of publishing this story. I would have bet money on it. And Lou, ever the old bulldog, refused.

The fallout from the Ashley Gibson story was swift. City leaders, including Sonya Hartman, called for both Lou and Tucker to be fired for compromising the Angel Baby investigation. Lou went into battle and came out mostly victorious; Tucker Renny was moved to general assignment reporter rather than fired, leaving the investigative reporter role open for me to eventually take.

I sighed, missing Lou. He was my boss, my mentor, and my friend – and Todd Waterman couldn't hold a candle to him. *I hope he's enjoying retirement in Florida,* I thought.

My phone buzzed. I picked it up and saw Nicholas' name on the screen, accompanied by a short, simple message: Call me. My stomach dropped. Our call the previous night hadn't gone all that great, and I was sure he now wanted to talk about it. I sighed and took another drink of wine to steel my nerves, then called him.

Nicholas answered on the first ring. "Hey you," he said.

"Hey."

"You hung up pretty quickly last night. Is everything okay?"

What I probably should have said: *No. Everything is not okay. My family is living in fear, never knowing when your family will show up and beat the information they want out of us. Would you be okay if you were in my shoes?*

What I actually said: "Sorry about that. I was in the middle of nowhere, must have lost signal. What's up?" I asked.

"I just wanted to see how you're doing. And I want to know what's going on. I get the feeling that something's changed between us."

I did not want to have this conversation right now. Not in the least. "Listen, I –"

"No, *you* listen, Rae." The anger in Nicholas' voice shocked me into shutting up. "I know you and your family are having a tough time right now. But don't you dare lump me into my grandfather's bullshit. I'm trying to *help* you. After eleven fucking years of listening to me denounce my grandfather and everything he stands for, I would think you'd know better."

Hot shame crawled up my neck and cheeks. "I –"

"*You* are my first priority, Raegan. You always have been. Until the other day, I thought you felt the same way."

I couldn't let this pass. "Yeah, well, the other day you did not, in fact, make me your priority. And my father was the one who paid the price. I'm not sure how you think things are going to be roses after that, Nicholas."

Silence on the other end of the line; my words hung between us like lead weights. I guzzled a bit more wine, hoping to calm my pounding heart.

"I'm sorry." For the first time, Nicholas' apology sounded genuine, and my heart broke a little. "I'm doing the best I can, babe. I'm in a tough spot here."

I sighed. "I get it. I do. I–I just don't know how we move forward from here."

"What do you mean?" His voice could have cut granite.

"I mean, you've done a great job of keeping Edison off our backs during the time we've been together. We've never really had to choose between us and our families. I don't know why, but things have changed now. Edison kidnapped my father, for god's sake. It is, and I'm sure will continue to be, really hard to keep the focus on us when everyone in your family is actively threatening my family."

"We've come this far, Raegan. We can't let my grandfather tear us apart." Was that a tinge of panic in Nicholas' voice?

"I–I'm just tired." I didn't realize how true those words were until they were out of my mouth. I set my glass on the table. "I'm tired and sad and worried and scared for my family."

"Do you worry about me as much as you worry about your family?"

I blinked. There was a chill in his voice that I'd never heard before. It made my stomach twist. "What do you mean? Of course I do."

"Then you should try a little harder to make me your priority."

For a second I thought I might throw up. *What is happening?* I wondered helplessly. Then I said, "I have to go, Nicholas. I'll talk to you later." I had to put some effort into my next words. "I love you."

"Do you?" he asked, and was gone.

I let my phone fall away from my ear and land on the loveseat cushion next to me. My laptop sat forgotten on my legs and my eyes burned with tears as I stared at the photo of my mom on the wall. My relationship with Nicholas was in real trouble.

But my family was also in real trouble. And no matter what guilt trip Nicholas tried to send me on, they came first. Bright anger obliterated all thought for a brief moment, and I chucked a throw pillow as hard as I could at the chair across the room. It landed harmlessly. Then I grabbed the half-full glass of wine on the table and downed it in one gulp. Big emotions swirled inside me, and this was the only way I knew how to cope with them.

I retrieved the bottle from the kitchen, sat back down on the loveseat, pulled my feet under me, and cradled it like a baby. I didn't even bother with a glass as I set myself on the fast track to blessed unconsciousness.

The last thing I saw before the alcohol finally smothered all conscious thought was my mother's smiling face on the wall — and I could have sworn I saw reproach in her eyes.

Wednesday, July 14, 2021

CHAPTER 12

I'd suffered many hangovers during my lengthy career as a high-functioning alcoholic, but perhaps none so severe as the one I woke up with on Wednesday morning. I was sprawled on the back porch loveseat, still dressed, gloves still on, covered with one of Mimi's afghan blankets. Lord, my head hurt. My whole *body* hurt. Every joint and every muscle had been injected with tiny shards of glass. I had to pry my tongue from the roof of my mouth just so I could groan.

I took a deep breath, exhaling fumes that could kill a small animal, and risked cracking an eye open. The sun wasn't up yet, but judging by the color of the sky outside the windows, it would be soon. The simple act of turning my head sent lightning bolts into my brain, and I groaned again. A glass of water and two aspirin sat on the table; left by Mimi, no doubt. It was a herculean effort to sit up and swallow the pills down, then guzzle all of the water. It wasn't enough to quench my thirst. I needed more.

I threw back the blanket and forced myself to stand. My sour stomach rolled, and for a panicky second I thought I was going to throw up. I closed my eyes and took deep breaths until the nausea subsided, then slowly shuffled into the kitchen. I poured a fresh glass of water, sipping it this time. I felt close to death.

A foil-covered pan of brownies sat on the counter. In the fridge were several storage containers with leftover pot roast and root vegetables. My family had enjoyed my favorite meal for dinner and I'd missed all of it, passed out drunk on the back porch.

My stomach turned again, this time with pure shame. I ran to the bathroom and threw up a mixture of water, acid and old wine. The smell, like rancid vinegar, triggered my gag reflex and I vomited over and over until there was nothing left. I sat on the cool bathroom floor, panting, sweating, and feeling like my insides had been wrung like a giant washrag. But I felt a little better.

A hot shower and some strong coffee helped bring me partway back to the land of the living. Nibbling on a brownie helped too. The hangover fog lifted just enough and I thought about my phone call with Nicholas the night before. *You should try a little harder to make me your priority,* he'd said. As angry as those words made me, I thought we'd finally had a breakthrough. Was I seeing a different side of Nicholas? Our circumstances, which reduced our relationship to a long series of texts and booty calls, would have made it easy for him to conceal his real self from me. The idea that I might have been bamboozled by a Faust and wasted over a decade of my life was too upsetting, so I closed my eyes and willed myself to stop thinking about it. When I opened my eyes again, the digital clock on the oven came into focus; I was going to be late for coffee with Hendricks if I didn't hurry.

The drive north was smooth with relatively light traffic, but I was driving with a hangover and a short fuse. I flipped the bird at an unsuspecting old lady in an old brown sedan who merged too closely in front of me, forcing me to tap the brakes. Even the Hits Morning Show served up nothing but nerve-grating noise, so I turned the radio off and drove in silence until I pulled up in front of the coffee shop at five minutes before eight.

Beananza was housed in an old repurposed gas station on the corner of Bridge Street and Marks Avenue, just north of Greenhaven Road and within walking distance of the RJPD. The whole place had a funky, almost gauche vibe to it: the exterior was clad in refurbished white stucco; large potted plants encased the small outdoor patio; and big pink metal flamingoes stood sentry on either side of the roll-up garage door. Inside, the small space was just as gaudy, featuring loud damask wallpaper, ostentatious chandeliers, photos of B-list celebrities in ornate frames, and what appeared to be an antique display case in one corner filled with a curious collection of women's shoes. The air was ripe with the aroma of freshly roasted and ground coffee beans. My mouth started to water.

Jesse Hendricks sat at a small two-person table next to the display case, staring out the window. He wore khakis and a green polo shirt, and his sidearm was prominent on his right hip. I pulled out the chair opposite him and sat. "Hey."

His eyes, accentuated by his green shirt, brightened when he saw me. His brow furrowed a bit when he realized my condition. "Feeling all right?"

"Been better," I admitted. "But coffee will help."

Hendricks stood. "What can I get for you?"

I tried to protest, but he would hear none of it. So I gave him my order and waited. Within minutes he was back with a steaming cup of life elixir; one sip of the strong, smooth bitterness helped inject a little more life into me.

Hendricks gave me a wry smile. "Better?"

I inhaled deeply of the coffee's fragrant steam, then let the air out slowly through my nose. "Yes. Much better. Thanks."

"Want to talk about it?"

I very nearly blurted out the entire sordid Nicholas story; something in Hendricks' kind eyes and open face made me want to unload my burdens onto him. *He's going to make a great detective,* I thought. *Nobody will be able to resist confessing their crimes to him.* But I didn't think Hendricks would think much of my relationship with Edison Faust's grandson, so I held back. "There's nothing to talk about. A little too much wine last night, is all."

He gazed directly into my soul for a moment, then shrugged. "All right then."

"How was your evening?" I asked, desperate to divert his attention away from me.

He shrugged again. I sensed a certain intensity about him this morning. "Fine. Nothing special. Spent most of it thinking about Mia."

"This case is important to you, isn't it?"

He sipped his coffee. "Yeah."

I thought about my brief vision of Hendricks and his mom receiving bad news from a sheriff's deputy. I was dying of curiosity and decided now was as good a time as any to try and get him to talk about that. "So what made you decide to become a cop?"

Hendricks frowned and fiddled with his coffee cup. He was quiet for a long time. I was about to repeat the question when he finally spoke. "Sometimes terrible things happen, things you don't mean, and you spend the rest of your life trying to make up for them."

Tread carefully, O'Rourke. "Did something terrible happen to you?"

Hendricks kept his eyes on his coffee cup, and his frown deepened. "Yes. Well, if I'm being honest, I caused something terrible to happen."

I didn't dare speak, but I watched his face closely.

He took a deep breath. "When I was seventeen years old, my girlfriend Amanda was killed in a car crash."

I gasped. "Oh no. I'm –"

Hendricks held up a hand. "Don't apologize. Please."

I shut up.

"She was on her way home from babysitting her sister's kids up in Saint Francis, driving on Highway 47. That's a two-lane highway the whole way. She crossed the centerline on a curve and hit a minivan head-on. She was killed instantly, and the other driver died before they got him to the hospital."

I winced.

"I believe Amanda crossed the centerline that night because she was upset and distracted. I–well, I'd broken up with her over the phone not two hours before her crash."

"How long had you been together?"

"Three years."

I winced again. "Oh, Jesse."

"I loved Amanda. I did. But there was this other girl, Camille Fontenot. She was beautiful. Exotic. Every guy in my high school wanted her, and I'd found out she was interested in me. I–ah, well, I wanted to see if I had a chance. I thought I could always go back to Amanda if it didn't work out."

I blinked several times. *What the fuck is the matter with teenage boys?* I wondered.

Hendricks' head fell even further and his face turned red. "Her parents sent a sheriff's deputy to my house to break the news. I think they knew what I'd done and couldn't face me themselves."

That was the vision I'd seen. I touched his hand with my gloved one. "You didn't cause her crash, Jesse."

"No, but I might as well have. If I hadn't broken up with her when I did, and the way I did, she would be alive right now. There is no doubt in my mind. Maybe she would have forgiven me for being a jackass kid and we'd be happily married today. Instead she's buried in the Hagen family plot at Hillside Cemetery." He looked at me with red-rimmed eyes. "And I'm the one who put her there."

I wanted to argue with him. I wanted to make him understand that he wasn't responsible for Amanda's crash. But I could see that it would be a waste of words, so instead I said, "And that's why you became a cop?"

"It was either find a way to make up for what I'd done, or let it consume me and probably kill myself. So I went into law enforcement. I wanted to help people."

"Is that what you always wanted to do?"

Another long silence. Then: "Before Amanda died, I was a musician. I played guitar in a band, and we had a big future ahead of us. We were starting to play some of the bigger venues in Minneapolis, and we were even talking to an agent." He paused. "Sometimes Amanda would sing with us. Her voice was amazing.

Like an angel." He spoke of her like she'd died twenty hours ago, not twenty years ago.

"Do you still play?" I asked, thinking that music might help him heal.

Hendricks shook his head. "I haven't picked up a guitar since that day."

I sat back in my chair and watched him continue to fidget with his coffee cup. This man had taken self-punishment to an entirely new level. He took full responsibility for the death of his girlfriend and then spent every single day of his life torturing himself in some twisted version of repentance. He'd never forgiven himself, and never allowed himself to heal. I suspected that behind that "good cop" façade lived a man who would have nothing to live for if not for his job. I worried what might happen if he didn't get this promotion to detective.

"Playing music might help you feel better," I offered.

He shook his head. "Music brings up bad memories."

He was stubborn about his self-torture, it seemed. "Okay," I said, giving up.

He sat for another quiet moment, composing himself, and then changed the subject. "How about you? How does an Ainsley get into investigative journalism?"

I shrugged and drank more coffee. "My reasons aren't so different from yours. I wanted to use my touch to help people. I originally planned to do TV news, but because I have a family of psychopaths after me, I chose the newspaper instead. It's easier to stay under Edison Faust's radar if my face isn't plastered all over the TV every night."

"Makes sense," Hendricks said.

"It ended up being a good choice. I turned out to be a pretty damn good writer, and I had an amazing boss who was also a fantastic mentor."

"Your touch must have come in really handy."

"Sure did. I always beat the competition to the big stories, and earned myself a reputation. Every news reporter in the Twin Cities – TV, radio, newspaper, didn't matter – wanted to *be* me."

"Sounds awesome. Why would you quit that?" Hendricks drank from his battered coffee cup.

I shrugged. "After the Catclaw Kids case, I realized I could use my touch to help people in a more meaningful way. I can give grieving families the answers they desperately seek. There is nothing more satisfying than that. I completely understand why you want to be a detective."

Hendricks hesitated, then said, "I imagine your touch has been more of a curse than a gift for your family. I mean, that's why you're always looking over your shoulder, right?"

I nodded.

"Do you think doing the PI thing and helping people is your way of making up for the bad things the touch has brought upon your family?"

I stared at him as it dawned on me: I too had spent my entire life under the shadow of something bad, trying to find my way into the sunlight. The touch had robbed my family of any happiness, stability, and comfort – and I wanted to use it to lessen other people's burdens. My own twisted version of repentance.

I sat back in my chair. "Damn, Hendricks. That's deep."

"But not wrong."

"No, definitely not wrong." I sighed. "I guess we're both just tortured souls, huh?"

He reached across the table, took my gloved hand in his, and squeezed. The warmth of his skin seeped through the thin leather covering mine. My heart raced, but the smile I gave him was confident as I squeezed back.

"We'll get there," Hendricks said, and released my hand.

"I hope so." I pulled my phone from my purse and checked the time. I was shocked to discover that nearly two hours had passed. "Think it's too early to track down Tom McCarthy?"

Hendricks stood. "I called him yesterday afternoon. He's expecting us."

I also stood and slung my purse over my shoulder. "Let's do it."

I stopped at the counter on my way out for a coffee to go. It was that kind of hangover.

CHAPTER 13

The Rummery was a modern dining room and bar housed in a renovated midcentury building on Hughes Street, which was one block off and ran parallel to Bridge Street. Hughes Street was lined with several other bars and restaurants, most of them tucked into stately late 19th-century brown brick buildings. The Rummery, with its copious glass, sleek lines, and faux leather seating, seemed proud of being different from the rest of the hole-in-the-wall establishments along Hughes.

The Rummery wasn't open for business yet, but Hendricks tried the copper-clad front door anyway and found it unlocked. We entered a dimly lit portico, walked past an abandoned host stand, and followed a short hallway that ran past the gleaming stainless steel kitchen. The scent of raw onions tickled my nose; the restaurant's cooks were just beginning to prep for lunch service.

Hendricks knocked on the half-open door at the end of the hallway, and the kind of deep voice that could weaken the knees of any red-blooded woman responded. "Hey, Jesse. Come on in."

Hendricks motioned for me to follow him, and we stepped into a fluorescent-lit, windowless room that looked like it belonged in a government building rather than a fancy restaurant.

The walls were painted a sterile off-white, and the enormous L-shaped oak desk that took up most of the space looked like it had time-traveled here from 1991. I had honestly expected something much more extravagant – leather couches and a wet bar, perhaps – from the owner of a place like this.

Tom McCarthy stood up and Hendricks shook his hand across the desk. This definitely was the man from yesterday's iron horse vision, and he had aged a lot in eleven years. His wispy blond hair, now white at the temples, had been combed and gelled just so in an effort to mask the fact that it was thinning. Deep lines framed his mouth.

His downturned basset hound eyes were his most remarkable feature. Their gorgeous shade of blue had not come across in the vision. The blue golf shirt he wore made me want to swim in those eyes like the ocean on a calm summer day. I introduced myself and shook his hand, and tried not to linger when we made eye contact.

McCarthy gestured toward the two chairs situated in front of his desk; Hendricks and I sat, then McCarthy took his seat. McCarthy glanced at me, then leveled his gaze on Hendricks. "So you want to talk about Mia."

"Yes. The River Junction Police Department is taking another look at her case, and your name has come up in a couple of conversations. Just have a few questions for you."

McCarthy made a sound through his nose. "I'm sure you heard that Mia and I had an affair."

"That did come up, yes," Hendricks acknowledged.

"Who told you that, I wonder?"

Hendricks shook his head. "I'm afraid I can't say."

McCarthy sat back in his chair, placed his right ankle on his left knee, and contemplated us with his cerulean eyes. I could not stop staring. "Well, it wasn't a very well-kept secret. I guess there were a handful of people who knew, or suspected. Thank god one of them wasn't my wife."

"When did this affair occur?" Hendricks asked.

McCarthy thought for a few seconds. "Ah, it started in May or June of two thousand nine, and ended that October."

I did the math in my head; if Tom McCarthy was telling the truth, he couldn't be Isabel's father. I wondered who was.

"Tell me more," Hendricks said.

"There's not much to tell. Mia worked for me for a couple of years. I knew she was something special the first day I met her. It started with some harmless flirting and rather quickly progressed to a full-on affair. I couldn't stop myself. She was irresistible."

"Even though you're married?" I gave McCarthy my very best wide-eyed Irish girl expression.

He nodded slowly. "Even though." He sighed. "I knew it was wrong. She just…well, she made me feel special. Like I was the only one who mattered. I don't get that from my wife anymore. Mia had a huge heart, and goddamn, she was smart. We would make love, then hold each other and just talk. We'd talk about politics, religion, everything. And the sex? Mindblowing." A short, sad pause. "I don't get that from my wife anymore, either."

Then why are you still married? I wondered, but did not say.

"She wanted me to leave my wife and start a new life with her. Hell, I wanted that too. We talked a lot about what a life together might look like."

"Did you leave your wife?" I asked.

"Ah, no. I just couldn't do that to my kids."

And there we have it. "Staying in a marriage for the kids": philanderer's code for toying with a young woman's emotions for his own sexual gratification, with no intention of ever leaving his marriage. There was no shortage of narcissistic jerks out there, and I was beginning to think Tom Blue Eyes here was one of them.

"How did Mia take it when you told her that?" Hendricks asked, making notes in his little notebook.

McCarthy hesitated.

"You did tell her, didn't you?" I asked.

"Yeah, I told her. And no, she didn't take it well."

"How did that go down?" Hendricks continued to write in his notebook, deliberately avoiding eye contact with McCarthy.

"I got spooked, all right? My wife busted me getting home late one night after I'd been with Mia. She seemed to buy my shitty excuse, but I was paranoid after that. I had to stop seeing Mia."

"How did that work?" I asked. "Seeing as how she worked for you."

"I kept an eye on her schedule and made it a point to not be here when she was working. It didn't matter; she called me on my cell all the time at first, wanting to know when I was coming over, what was wrong, what did she do, all that emotional chick crap. So finally one evening I stopped by her house and told her I was staying with my wife and she and I were done."

"What was her reaction?" Hendricks' voice could have shaved ice.

"She screamed and threw a statue at me," McCarthy said. "It looked like a horse and it was damn heavy. Left a gash on my arm that took weeks to heal."

That was a vision I wanted to see. I made a mental note to spend a little more time with Mia's iron horse figurine.

"Did she continue to work for you?" Hendricks asked, his tone still frosty.

"Yeah. I expected she'd quit, but goddamned if she didn't stick around. I tried to avoid her, but it was hard. The first couple weeks after our breakup she was always here, and always trying to talk to me about getting back together." He chuckled mirthlessly. "When that didn't work, she started coming into the restaurant on her days off with these random guys. She'd drink too much, laugh too loud, get real handsy with them. She was trying to make me jealous."

"Did it work?" I asked.

"At first, yeah," McCarthy admitted. "But then she just seemed desperate."

She probably was, I thought. *Women with broken hearts will do anything to stop the bleeding.*

"She was still working here when she went missing," Hendricks pointed out. "You and she must have figured something out."

"She eventually gave up on me," McCarthy said. "But I worried about her. She was drinking a lot and I heard she was sleeping around."

"Who did you hear that from?" Hendricks asked.

McCarthy shrugged. "My staff talks. Mia's best friend worked here too. Jenna Spitzer. She and Jenna were tight as could be."

Hendricks raised his eyebrows, then made a note. "One last question. Where were you the day Mia went missing?"

Surprised, McCarthy put his foot back on the ground and sat back in his chair. "What – you don't think –"

Hendricks held up a hand. "Just answer the question, please."

McCarthy thought for a second or two, then said, "Well, I remember the delivery truck came at like seven o'clock that morning. A full two hours earlier than usual, and the dipshit driver couldn't even give me a decent excuse." He shook his head. "Jenna was the only one I could convince to come and help me unload. After that I probably went to the gym, and then I went home." He offered the names of a few people who could vouch for him, including his wife. "If you talk to her, please don't tell her about Mia." His pleading azure eyes moved from Hendricks to me and back again.

Hendricks stood and offered his hand. "Thank you for your time today, Tom. We'll see ourselves out."

We said our goodbyes and left a slightly befuddled Tom McCarthy in his office. We walked through furnace-like heat to the RJPD and settled into our air-conditioned war room. Hendricks left briefly to retrieve a cold bottle of water for each of us. I guzzled mine, still parched from last night's wine extravaganza.

He picked up the desk phone and called down to the records tech on duty. "Laura, I need a current phone number for Jenna Spitzer." He paused, then said, "Sorry, her name is Talbot now." He jotted something in his notebook. "Thanks, Laura. Appreciate you." He pressed the plunger on the phone's base to end the call, then immediately released the plunger to reopen the line and dialed Jenna Talbot's number. "Hi Jenna, it's Jesse Hendricks, how –" A pause. "I know, it's been a long time. Listen, I'm investigating Mia Masterson's disappearance, and I –" Jenna interrupted him with a lengthy diatribe; to me, listening from the outside, she sounded like a chattering chipmunk. "Yes, me too," Hendricks said. "I was wondering if I could stop by and ask you some questions." A pause. "Okay, will you be home tomorrow? Great. See you then." He hung up and looked at me. "Jenna and I went to high school together."

"What did you think of Tom McCarthy?" I asked.

Hendricks stood and went to the whiteboard. "Your typical douchebag," he said and uncapped a marker. "I feel bad for his wife." Then he added McCarthy to the growing web surrounding Mia Masterson on the board.

Exhaustion, the result of drinking entirely too much the night before and not getting any quality sleep at all, hit me like a freight train. Suddenly I needed to prop my head up for fear it might break off my neck and roll away, and the simple act of keeping my eyelids open felt like an epic battle.

"Raegan?" I forced myself to look up; Hendricks watched me from where he stood, concern clear on his face.

"I'm sorry. I – I'm not feeling well," I admitted.

Hendricks capped his marker and sat next to me. "You shouldn't drive. Let me take you home."

"What about my car?" I asked, eyes closed.

"If you leave me your keys, I'll move it into the PD lot. It's fenced and there are cameras. I'll pick you up in the morning, and maybe I'll even bring you a coffee."

It was an offer I couldn't refuse. "Thank you, Jesse. I appreciate it."

I spent the ride home trying to stay awake enough to navigate Hendricks to my dad's house. To his credit, Hendricks left me alone and didn't ask any questions.

Kieran was mowing the front lawn when Hendricks pulled into the driveway. He looked at the unmarked cruiser suspiciously, then stopped the mower and walked over when I got out of the car.

"Everything all right?" he asked, giving me a head-to-toe once-over.

"Fine," I said. "Kieran, this is Jesse Hendricks. He's the officer I'm working with on the case in River Junction. Jesse, this is my brother Kieran. He's in town from Eugene, Oregon for a while. Now, if you'll both excuse me, I need to go lie down. Thanks for the ride, Jesse." I left them standing in the driveway.

Mimi was in the living room watching her soap operas. I mumbled a quick hello as I shuffled past on my way to my room. I closed the door behind me and crawled under the covers. Every muscle in my body seemed to sigh with relief as I stretched out on my bed.

When my mother left us, she promised me that she would visit me every night in my dreams, and she generally kept that promise on the nights I didn't drink myself unconscious. I hadn't seen her in several nights. She didn't show up to our last dream-rendezvous, and I suspected she was angry with me for prioritizing my relationship with Nicholas over my family's safety.

Turned out she was right to be angry. My stupidity got my dad hurt. I sighed deeply, and a tear sneaked its way out from beneath a closed eyelid. It left a wet track across my temple.

I finally fell asleep – and my mother came to see me.

PART 2:
NICHOLAS

Thursday, July 15, 2021

CHAPTER 14

We always met at the same park bench in the same beautiful dream-park. I didn't have to wait very long. Danielle, looking exactly as she did the day she got into the family car and drove away in September of 1989, appeared and walked toward me. She was smiling, her face serene — but her snapping hazel eyes betrayed that serenity. She was not happy with me.

"Hi Mom," I said.

Danielle sat on the bench next to me. Her tight shoulder-length blonde curls moved with the breeze. She stared at the grass at her feet and didn't say anything. My dream-mom was normally so content and ethereal — this was not like her. At all.

"I'm sorry," I offered. The apology felt wildly inadequate, but I had to say something. I couldn't stand her silence.

Danielle shook her head and looked at me. The anger in her eyes had fallen away, replaced with deep sadness. "You're going to have to make a choice, Rae."

I involuntarily sucked air in through my nose; she might as well have sucker-punched me right in the gut. "You think I should break things off with Nicholas, don't you?"

"I think you've gotten yourself into a terrible situation, baby. You can't have it both ways. Somebody's going to get hurt."

"Somebody already has," I muttered.

She touched my hand; we were both gloveless and carefree in my dreams.

"How long have you known about Nicholas?" I asked. All this time I thought I'd done such a fabulous job of keeping my secret from my dream-mother.

"I've always known, baby."

I sighed. "He's not a bad person, Mom. He's not like his grandfather." The words sounded trite to my own ears.

"Are you sure about that, baby?" Her eyes were now wide and probing.

"I was," I said miserably. "I'm not so sure since Dad got hurt."

"I think you know what you need to do." Danielle slipped an arm around my shoulders and gave me a side-hug. Then she stood.

"Kieran wants you to come home," I blurted before she could turn and leave me.

The smile she gave me was so radiant, so beautiful. Angelic. "I know, baby."

"I don't know if you should," I said.

"It's all right, baby. I can't wait to see you."

My breath caught in my throat. "Does that mean you're coming home? For real?"

"I have to go, baby. I love you." Danielle moved away from me as if on wheels. "I'll see you soon." She blew me a kiss and was gone.

∞

A soft knocking noise pulled me out of unconsciousness. My eyes popped open and stared into the darkness of my childhood bedroom. My heart pounded in my throat and I held my breath, hoping it had been part of my dream. I glanced at the clock and groaned inwardly at the time: 2:12 a.m.

There was the knocking noise again, and I realized it was coming from my window. Heavy drapes designed to block sunlight and nosy lookie-loos from seeing inside meant I couldn't see what – or who – was outside either. I shot out of bed, ran on the balls of my feet to the other side of the room, and flipped the lightswitch. I squinted against the sudden brightness and hoped that the light would scare the window-knocker away.

Nope. A third knock sounded, louder and more insistent, as if the light had actually emboldened them. I turned the light off again and crossed the room; my fear had morphed into anger, and I was prepared to give this inconsiderate jackass a piece of my mind. I swept the curtain aside, peered through the window, and found myself nearly nose-to-nose with a pale, disembodied face. I jumped back and nearly screamed.

A pale finger appeared and pressed against the face's lips, as if telling me to be quiet. That's when I finally realized who was standing outside my bedroom window at two o'clock in the morning.

It was Nicholas.

Panting, my heart racing in my chest, I slid my window open. Humid night air poured in. "Nicholas? What are you doing here?" I whispered. Did he know I was staying here? And had I ever told him where my dad lived? I couldn't remember.

"Let me in," he whispered back. "We need to talk. I have some updates for you."

"Are you kidding me? It's two o'clock in the fucking morning. I was *sleeping*." I didn't think I'd ever sleep again after the scare he'd just given me.

"I know, I'm sorry. Edison has had me staying at the Fortress, and this was the only time I could get out."

"You've been in River Junction?" This was interesting. As far as I knew, Nicholas' policy was to spend as little time with his grandfather as possible. And the fact that he hadn't mentioned this little detail in our last phone conversations was even more interesting. "Meet me at the front door."

I tiptoed through the dark and quiet house. *What the hell are you doing, O'Rourke? You're going to let a Faust into your father's house?* I had enough good sense left to know that was a terrible idea. So I made a game-time decision and stuck my feet into Liam's slippers, which he kept in the front entry and wore to retrieve his morning newspapers, unlocked the front door, and stepped outside.

The night air was warm and humid, threatening to transform my curls into pure frizz. Nicholas stood on the threshold, clad in a black t-shirt and black gym shorts. *No wonder I couldn't see anything but his face,* I thought. His rumpled black hair had also fallen victim to the humidity.

He stepped forward, expecting to be led into the house. I closed the door and said, "We can talk out here."

It was too dark to see his face clearly, but he seemed a little taken aback. "Um, okay." Then he gathered me into a big hug, burying his face in my hair. "God, I've missed you."

I closed my eyes and hugged him back. The odor of cigar smoke clung to him. I heard my dream-mother's voice: *I think you know what you need to do.*

Nicholas released me and softly kissed me. He tasted like cigars and whiskey. Then he held my face in his hands and examined me closely. His black eyes were nearly invisible in the dark. "How are you? Okay?"

Not really, I thought, but I nodded anyway. "I'm fine."

"I was hoping we could talk inside. And maybe…you know…" His arms slipped around my waist again and pulled my body against his.

The thought of having sex with Nicholas in my dad's house, especially after our last disastrous phone call, made my stomach turn. *Do you worry about me as much as you worry about your family?* he'd asked. "It's not going to happen, Nicholas. I'm sure you can understand why. How did you know I was here?"

Nicholas let me go and stepped back. "You told me. Remember? You said you weren't going back to your apartment after Morgan ransacked it and would be staying with your dad for awhile."

Had I? I didn't remember saying that, but I supposed it was possible; the last few days had been really hectic. I had one more clarifying question. "When did I tell you where he lived, though?"

Nicholas hesitated, then said, "Ah, you didn't."

Then I realized: "Morgan told you." Morgan, who had stalked my father and then abducted him right out of his own driveway. My revulsion crept up in intensity and I moved another step back from Nicholas.

"I'm sorry," he said. "I–I just really needed to see you, Rae. Make sure you're okay."

"I said I'm fine," I snapped. I took a deep breath to calm myself, then said, "What else did you want to tell me?"

Nicholas's hands disappeared into the pockets of his shorts. "Edison summoned me to the Fortress after you stopped him and Morgan from beating your mother's whereabouts out of your father. I can't begin to describe how pissed he is."

I shrugged, strangely unintimidated by this. Maybe because I'd faced that crazy old man once already and not only survived, but triumphed. "Okay, and your point?"

"My point is, you all still have targets on your backs. Big ones. I've spent the last couple of days schmoozing with him, drinking bourbon, smoking more cigars than I honestly care to, and listening. I know what he's planning."

"Let's hear it," I said, and leaned against a pillar that supported the roof over my dad's front patio.

Nicholas did the same on the other side of the walk and crossed his arms over his muscular chest. Not too long ago I would have desperately wanted to run my hands over those pecs.

"First, it's important that you know he's in a bad way financially right now."

"Oh, and why's that?"

"Let's just say cryptocurrency is a young man's game."

I gazed thoughtfully at Nicholas' silhouette. "Another failed get-rich-quick scheme?"

"You got it. Which means he now has way more ground to make up in his quest to return the Fausts to their pre-World War Two wealth, glory, and status in River Junction. And you might have noticed he's no spring chicken."

I nodded, remembering Edison's wild gossamer hair, deeply wrinkled hawk-like face, and sensible shoes. No, he did not have much time left.

"So now he's cooked up a new plan. One that he believes is utterly foolproof."

"Can't wait to hear it." I couldn't quite keep the snark out of my voice.

Nicholas shifted his position slightly, leaning his other shoulder against the pillar now. "Okay. You're not a River Junction local, so you haven't heard of Jack Hughes."

I shook my head.

"Jack was a pretty regular guy who came from an old River Junction family. He graduated from River Junction High School in 1960. Same class as Edison, and they were best buddies – that is, until Arlene Callahan broke up with Edison during their senior year in high school and started dating Jack. Edison, naturally, did not take it well. He considered Jack his sworn enemy after that."

"Just another example of what happens when you piss off a Faust," I said scornfully.

Nicholas nodded. "No shit. Anyway, Jack went to work at the Ainsley Mill right out of high school, operating the grain elevators. He married Arlene Callahan in 1962, had a nice house close to the Bourbon River, and a pretty good life.

"But the thing about Jack was, he didn't trust the banks. Jack's father, Raymond, lost everything in the stock market crash of 1929. The bank ran out of money before he could withdraw his life's savings. Raymond and his family suffered for well over a decade. This all happened before Jack was born, but his father talked about it often and Jack took his experience to heart. If you don't put money in the bank, they can't keep it from you when times get tough. That was his philosophy."

"What did he do instead?" I asked, intrigued.

"He took his wages in cash, paid bills in cash, and converted the rest into gold coins. And then he stashed them away. That was his life savings. Or so the town rumor mill said."

"Did he stash them in a mattress?" I thought this was a pretty funny joke, but Nicholas didn't even crack a smile.

"Arlene died of breast cancer in 1992, and Jack became a recluse. He went to work and then he went home to Scout, his terrier mutt. He never went out. Jack was only fifty-five years old when he was found bludgeoned to death in 1997."

I winced. "What happened to all of his gold coins?"

Nicholas shrugged. "When the family cleaned out his house, there were none to be found. Not even in the mattress." I couldn't see his face very well, but I could hear a touch of humor in his voice. "I was in high school at the time and I remember the mystery of Jack Hughes' gold was all anyone could talk about. Some folks thought he buried them in his yard. Others thought they might be hidden at the Ainsley Mill somewhere. People have been looking ever since, and no trace of them has ever been found."

"Are we sure they exist?" I asked doubtfully.

"I don't think there's ever been any actual evidence that these gold coins exist. Nobody's ever seen them with their own eyes – but that doesn't seem to deter people. Citizens of River Junction have been digging holes all over town for almost twenty-five years."

"Okay, so let me guess. Edison wants this hidden trove of gold coins, and he thinks my mom can help him find it."

"Bingo," Nicholas said. "He swears that Jack Hughes' gold is hidden somewhere, and he believes that's what will finally put the Fausts back at the top of the food chain in River Junction."

It sounded so silly to me. Edison's fixation on his grandfather's grudge was so utterly pointless and destructive. What kind of a way was that to live?

"Do we know how many gold coins Hughes supposedly had?" I asked.

Nicholas shook his head. "No, but Edison believes there's a shitload."

"How does he think my mom can help him find them?" I finally knew the real answer to this question, and was curious if Nicholas knew too.

"He – ah, he had Morgan procure some of Jack's belongings from his brother."

I remembered something Jesse Hendricks said the day I first met him: *Nothing ever sticks. Not even when they beat an elderly couple to within an inch of their lives.* It took everything I had to stop myself from moving even farther away from Nicholas. "So the hope is that my mom will touch one of those items and see where Jack hid his gold," I said.

"Exactly."

I decided to play dumb. "It'll never work. Too much time has passed. There's nothing left for her to see."

"Edison is convinced she can do it. Ain't no way he's backing down from this plan. He's too desperate."

I dipped my head and scowled. "Well, it's a stupid plan." I looked up at him from below my furrowed brow. "What are you going to do to stop him?"

His entire body seemed to deflate. "I honestly don't think I can, Rae. Not this time."

Anger began to radiate from my chest. "You promised. Figure it out."

He didn't look at me, just stood there against the pillar with his hands in his pockets.

"I gotta go in. Good night, Nicholas."

I stepped inside the house before he could reply and closed the door behind me. Then I did something that until this moment I would never have even considered: I locked the door while Nicholas was still out there. The *click* noise the deadbolt made as it slid into the doorframe sounded so…final. It felt like a harbinger of things to come for Nicholas and me. It was becoming painfully clear that we weren't going to make it through this. It was only a matter of time.

I peeked through the sidelight and watched him walk slowly through the darkness, his way illuminated by a single street lamp at the end of the driveway. Then he climbed into his red Audi and drove away.

I spent the rest of the early hours tossing, turning, and worrying.

Was it really a good idea to bring Mom home now?

What was I going to do about Nicholas?

And what did Kieran tell Hendricks about me after I left them in the front yard?

CHAPTER 15

"Rae. Wake up."

I opened my eyes. A vague man-shaped blob stood in front of me. I blinked my gritty eyes until my brother came into focus. He looked like he'd just rolled out of bed in his boxers and basic white t-shirt. His copper hair was flat on one side and his ice blue eyes danced. "Wha? What time is it?"

"It's early. Five o'clock."

I groaned. "Damn it, Kieran, I just got back to sleep."

"Long night?"

I closed my eyes and pulled my blankets over my head with a petulant grunt. "Go away."

"You're going to want to get up, Rae."

I flipped the blankets off my head and glared at Kieran. "No, I really don't. I want to catch another hour or two of sleep before I have to go to work."

Kieran shrugged and took a few steps toward the door. "All right, suit yourself. I'll tell her you say hi."

Her? Every cell in my body went still. "What do you mean?"

He grinned. "Dad is video calling Mom as we speak."

My heart slammed against my ribcage and I sat up. "Shut up. Are you serious?"

"As a heart attack. Hurry up. We're in the dining room. Mimi's already got the coffee going."

I rolled out of bed, threw on whatever clothes I grabbed first, ran out to the kitchen to pour myself a cup of coffee, then beelined for the dining room. My family sat at one end of the long table, huddled around Liam's laptop with giant smiles on their faces.

"My goodness, I'm overwhelmed," the slightly reedy voice of a woman filled the room. "I can't – wait, where's Raegan?"

Kieran looked up, saw me, and gestured at me to hurry up and join them. "She's here, Mom."

I rounded the end of the table and bent over at the waist so my mother and I could see each other better. I expected to see the mother who visited me in my dreams. And I did, sort of – but the woman on the laptop screen was much older. Her golden curls had turned platinum, and wrinkles decorated the entirety of her careworn face – a face that had shades of Mimi's face and my own. The skin along her chin and neck hung a little more loosely. But her smile, oh, her smile was exactly as I remembered it, and my heart melted. I smiled at my mother – my actual, real-life mother – through hot tears. "Hi, Mom."

Danielle tried to suppress a sob and failed. "Hello, family."

We all laughed through our tears. Kieran wiped his blotchy face dry with his t-shirt. Mimi dabbed her eyes with a tissue. Even Liam was misty-eyed.

"I wish I could reach through this computer and hug you all," Danielle said, emotion roughening her voice to the point of cracking.

I wanted that more than anything. "Us too, Mom," I said.

"Is Uncle Carl taking care of you?" Kieran asked.

Danielle smiled. "Yes, baby, he's been wonderful. Makes sure I have everything I need."

"What do you do up there?" I asked. "All by yourself."

"Well, I paint a lot, and sculpt. I've developed a talent for nature photography, the country up here is absolutely stunning, and I make a little money selling the prints. I've made friends with some of the folks in Isabella – that's the closest town. Paula, she owns the general store, is my best friend. Uncle Carl stops by occasionally and we share a cup of tea."

At first I heard *Isabella* as *Isabel,* and Jesse Hendricks' face appeared in my mind's eye. Something in my gut turned warm & fuzzy.

"But mostly I think about you guys. Your dad and Mimi have been keeping me updated on your lives."

My dad pushed the laptop farther down the table so we could all pull up a chair. We talked for the longest time, about everything. Danielle asked Kieran about Annie and life in Oregon. Then she asked me about quitting the newspaper and going into business for myself. At first I was mildly shocked; I'd only just told my family about that a couple of days ago. Then I glanced at my dad, who was gazing at my mom's face on the screen with unabashed love. He talked to her much more often than we realized, it seemed.

"Your dad tells me you all are ready to bring this family back together again," Danielle said.

Everyone else glanced at each other with growing excitement, but I kept my widened eyes on my mother. My mind spun with everything I'd learned about her touch, and what Nicholas had told me the previous night about his grandfather's plan. I was more convinced than ever that bringing our mother home now was a bad idea. Doing so would only give Edison Faust the opportunity to take her away from us again. Forever this time.

No.

"What did you say, Rae?" I blinked and looked at Kieran, who was staring at me with wide, incredulous eyes.

"I didn't say anything," I said.

"I heard you very distinctly say 'No.'"

Did I? "Look, I'm just thinking maybe we –"

Kieran exploded. "Are you kidding me?" he shouted. "We talked about this! Being all together gives us strength and power in numbers. Or did you drink too much wine and suddenly you don't remember that conversation?"

"Kieran," Liam admonished him in a stern tone. "That was uncalled for."

He doesn't know how powerful her touch is. That was the only coherent thought I could muster before I snapped. I abruptly stood, nearly spilling my coffee. "Fuck you, Kieran!" I shouted. "At least I didn't abandon my fucking wife!"

"Raegan," my father turned his reproach to me, but I barely heard him. I was entirely too angry with – and hurt by – my brother.

"I was protecting her!" Kieran's not-insignificant voice was at full volume now. "Just like I'm trying to fucking protect YOU!"

"I don't need you to protect me! Bringing Mom home isn't going to keep us safe, Kieran! You have no idea the lengths Edison Faust will go to get his hands on her! She comes home and she becomes bait!"

"Oh, and you know all about Edison's nefarious plans?" Kieran's face devolved into an ugly sneer.

"Yes!" I screamed. My head pounded. "He wants to –" I realized what I was about to say and clamped my mouth shut.

The room fell silent and everyone stared at me. I slowly sat back in my chair and covered my face with my hands. *I fucked up.* I wanted to cry.

"He wants to what, exactly?" Kieran had lowered the volume but not the intensity of his voice.

I removed my hands from my face and looked at Kieran defiantly. "He wants to get his hands on Mom and use her touch. We all know that." *You just don't know all the details.* "And until the threat is neutralized, I think it's better for Mom to stay where she is." I sat back in my chair and crossed my arms over my chest.

Kieran was incredulous. "How in the hell do you go from all in on bringing Mom home to dead set against it in the span of forty-eight hours? How?"

Mimi finally decided to intervene. "That's enough. Both of you hush."

We hushed.

"We will continue to discuss this – as a family – when you two calm down, apologize to each other, and start behaving like adults." Mimi's eyes were on fire behind her glasses. It was a little unnerving; we didn't see her angry very often, and it wasn't an emotion that looked particularly at home on her grandmotherly face. "But ultimately the decision rests with Danielle and Liam. Do you both understand me?"

I dropped my head, feeling more than a little ashamed of myself. I was sure Kieran felt the same. "Yes," we said in unison.

"It's been hard. I know." My mother was still on the laptop screen, now dabbing her red and puffy eyes with a tissue. I noticed that she, too, wore lambskin gloves. "Kieran, Raegan, I want you both to know that I would never have left you if I felt I had a choice. I did what I had to do to keep us all as safe as possible. Okay? It's not a perfect plan, but it's worked. Until now. Edison kidnapped your dad, which tells me he's more motivated than he's ever been. They will eventually find me. It's only a matter of time. That means none of us are safe. The idea that we can be is laughable."

Hot tears pooled in my eyes. I knew she was right.

"Your mother and I are not going to make any rash decisions," Liam said. "But something has to and will change. In the meantime, this family must stick together. No more fighting. Understood?"

Kieran and I, again in unison: "Yes."

"I love you all," Danielle said, her voice breaking again.

This, on top of the extreme stress of the last two weeks, finally broke my dam. I laid my head in my folded arms and sobbed. A moment or two later an arm snaked across my back and a head laid on my shoulder. "I'm sorry, Rae." Kieran's voice, deep and shaky, murmured in my ear. "That was a low blow. I'm an asshole."

I couldn't have controlled my sobs if I'd tried, so I just let them come. I'd been riding a nonstop emotional rollercoaster since learning that my neighbors had lost their dog in a cabin fire up north. It was a life-changing moment, for sure – but it also triggered a wild series of ups and downs, triumphs and losses, joy and despair. It was a lot, and it had finally overwhelmed me.

I felt a gentle hand on my back and another, stronger hand on my other shoulder. The warmth and love my family shared with me through their touch calmed me, and my sobs finally settled into sniffles and hiccups. I raised my head, wiped my face with my own t-shirt, and said, "Love you too, Mom. I'm so glad I got to see for myself that you're all right. I –" My voice cracked. "I've missed you every single day since you left."

"Me too, baby." A sob escaped her too.

She promised we would see her regularly now that discussions about bringing her home were underway, and the call ended with all of us blowing her kisses, and her returning them with interest.

My Mimi, my dad, and my brother returned to their chairs, and we sat there looking at each other for a moment. Kieran finally broke the silence.

"That was hard."

We all agreed.

"It's not going to get easier, is it?"

I thought he meant this to be a hypothetical question, but Mimi gave him an answer anyway. "No. It isn't."

We all contemplated this, and then I looked at the little clock in the lower right corner of my dad's laptop screen. It was nearly seven-thirty. "Holy crap, it's been over two hours," I said. "I have to get ready for work."

Kieran ambushed me on my way out of the dining room, wrapping me in a big hug. "I really am sorry, Rae."

I hugged him back tightly. "I know you are, O'Rourke. I am too."

He released me and I threw the rest of my family a wave before heading for the shower. "I love you guys."

"Have a good day, Rae." My dad lifted his hand in return, and Mimi blew me a kiss.

It was seven-thirty in the morning and I was already exhausted. I wondered what else the day had in store for me.

CHAPTER 16

Hendricks had a big coffee for me when he picked me up at eight o'clock, my hair still wet from the shower and no makeup on my face. "Ah, thank you," I said.

Hendricks took one look at my face, and asked, "Are you okay?"

"I've had better mornings." I eagerly grabbed the coffee cup with its paper sleeve and breathed in the delicious aroma. "This will help."

We arrived at RJPD and settled into the war room. My coffee cup was like a baby's pacifier, never far away from my lips.

Hendricks stood looking at the whiteboard, absentmindedly tapping a marker against his teeth. "Thirty-two minutes," he muttered.

"What's that?" I took another sip of coffee.

He pointed. "James Locke saw Mia drive away from her house at seven forty-five on the morning of September twenty-second, and she made her last call thirty-two minutes later, at eight-seventeen."

"Right." I remembered talking about this the other day.

"Where did she go?" *Tic-tic-tic* went the marker against his teeth.

I set my empty coffee cup on the desk and propped my chin in my hand. "Well, that's pretty early on a–" I consulted my phone's calendar app "–Wednesday morning. What's open at that hour?"

Hendricks' eyebrows went up as he considered this. "Here in town? Not much. The hardware store for sure. Maybe the drugstore."

"Are they located in downtown River Junction?"

"As a matter of fact, they are. Hold on." He left the room and came back a couple minutes later with a wall map of River Junction. It was too big for the whiteboard, so he used some scrounged push pins to hang it directly on the wall. "Don't tell Captain Bailey." Then he dug in the desk for something else: small sticky flags, the kind used to mark important areas in documents.

"Your secret is safe with me," I said solemnly.

We stood shoulder to shoulder and examined the map. "This is Mia's house," Hendricks said, placing a sticky flag next to the intersection of Grove Street and Fourth Avenue, south of downtown. "This is the hardware store." He marked a spot on Bridge Street between Third and Fourth Avenues. "And the drugstore is here." He placed a flag at Bridge Street and Second Avenue.

I noticed something that let the air out of our fledgling theory. "All of those establishments are like a mile north of Mia's house. James Locke saw her driving south."

"That's right, he did." Hendricks squinted at the map. "What are we missing?"

144

"Maybe she didn't stay in River Junction," I offered. "Maybe she had an appointment in Minneapolis. Could've been for the baby, there's a children's hospital there."

"Maybe." Hendricks didn't sound convinced. "I don't know...I can't shake the feeling that she never left town."

"What makes you think that?"

He shrugged. "I don't know. Nothing concrete. Just a gut feeling."

A big sigh escaped me. "Think it might be worth talking to the people at those businesses?"

"At this point, anything's worth a shot." Hendricks pulled his notebook from his pocket and jotted down some names. "Lyle Allister is the pharmacist, he's been around forever. Lucy MacGraw, his pharmacy tech, was around back in twenty-ten also. And Pete Barker runs the hardware store."

I stood. "Great, let's do it."

Hendricks glanced at the clock. "Let's talk to Jenna first. She's on the west side of town, and we can swing by the pharmacy and the hardware store on our way back."

"Okay." I slung my purse over my shoulder. "Can we stop at Beananza?"

It was another two-coffee sort of day.

∞

Jenna Spitzer Talbot lived in an ancient two-story L-shaped house in a neighborhood west of Bridge Street. The clapboard exterior was painted a shade of gray that really only belonged on Navy submarines, and the bright purple trim was just offensive. Her vehicle, an old blue SUV with corroded doors and fenders, sat in a narrow gravel driveway next to the house. There was no garage; the house clearly predated the automobile by a couple of decades. A newer-looking air conditioner hummed in the lower of two narrow front windows. Piles of dogshit littered the patchy front yard, which was enclosed by a mangled chainlink fence.

"Nice house," I observed, holding my hot coffee cup close to my face and taking comfort from its warmth – even on this scorcher of a July day.

"I try not to judge," Hendricks said, throwing the car into park. "But sometimes it's easier said than done."

We got out and made our way to the front door, which was tucked in the corner where the house's two gables met. In some spots it looked to me like the cobwebs were all that was keeping the house from falling apart. Hendricks' knock made the rickety screen door rattle in its frame.

The door opened immediately, as if the person inside had watched us approach. Behind the screen door stood a woman who'd clearly had a rougher go at life than most. Jenna Talbot was thirty-nine years old, but she looked at least a decade older than that. Her dark brown hair, with badly damaged bleached ends, was piled on top of her head and mostly held in place with a velvet scrunchie. Her eyebrows had been drawn on her pudgy face and her eyelids were caked with aggressive black eyeliner, giving her a slightly sinister appearance despite her wide, gap-toothed smile. A fading bruise ringed her right eye and stretched across the bridge of her flattened nose. She wore yoga pants that had faded to a dirty gray, and an oversized River Junction High School t-shirt that stretched over her generous bosom and ass. She held a lit cigarette between two fingers of her right hand. "Jesse!" she cried in a smoke-roughened voice.

Hendricks smiled. "Jenna, it's nice to –"

Jenna stepped outside, pulling the front door closed behind her. "Nope, nope, I'm a hugger. Come here, you big lug." She forced Hendricks into a one-armed hug, careful to keep the lit cigarette away from him.

He gingerly patted her back, then stepped away from her. I couldn't blame him; the odor of smoke, fresh on top of stale, hung around her like a thick fog. A closer look at her face revealed a slightly yellow tint to her skin and deep vertical wrinkles around her lips – smoker's lines, Mimi had called them once. I had an idea that she spent her days holed up in the house, chain smoking and watching soap operas. I didn't see any evidence of kids in the yard, thank god; any kid who showed up to school smelling like Jenna Talbot did was in for merciless teasing.

Jenna took a deep drag from her cigarette and flicked the smoldering butt into the yard. "Do you guys want to come in?" she rasped. "I got Cokes in the fridge."

Hendricks drew his little notebook and pen from the pocket of his khaki pants. "Thank you, but no. We can't stay long." He gestured at me. "This is Raegan O'Rourke, she's working with me on the investigation into Mia's disappearance."

Jenna gave me the briefest of glances. "Nice to meet you." And then she returned her full attention to Hendricks. I got the feeling she had a bit of a thing for him. Maybe even since high school.

"How has life been treating you, Jenna?" As if he didn't already know the answer.

She pulled a battered pack of Camels from the pocket of her yoga pants and lit one with a red Bic lighter. "I kicked Wade out."

Hendricks frowned. "I can't believe you stayed with him as long as you did."

Jenna shrugged. "What can I say, fucker always knows what to say to wiggle his way back into my life. Although last week he broke my nose and damn near put me in the hospital. See?" She pointed at the bruise on her face. "Grade-A asshole, is what he is. I'm fucking done. I even made him come get that piece of shit Mustang out of my fucking driveway."

"You be careful," Hendricks said. "Sometimes assholes like Wade don't take no for an answer."

Jenna waved the hand holding her cigarette. "He's got a new woman. Alisa Bennett? Remember her?"

Hendricks nodded slowly. "I do. Vaguely. Blonde hair, kinda quiet?"

"That's her," Jenna said. "His Mustang is in her garage now, over at the Royal Oaks apartments. She can fucking have him." She took a drag and exhaled a plume of blue smoke. A dog barked from behind the front door, and it sounded large. "Shut UP!" she shouted over her shoulder, then gave us an irritated look. "I swear, one of these days I'm gonna drop that fucking mutt off at the animal shelter."

"Are you working?" Hendricks inquired.

Jenna shook her head. "I'm on disability. Wrecked my back five years ago, thanks to a dumbass dishwasher at the Rummery who left a puddle on the floor and I slipped in it. Tom McCarthy can go fuck himself for fighting my worker's comp claim." She dragged again and started hacking. Her coughs had a deep phlegmy quality that made me think she would likely be tethered to an oxygen tank in a few short years.

Hendricks waited for Jenna to compose herself, then said, "We just spoke with Tom yesterday. He says you and Mia were pretty close."

"We were besties," Jenna said simply.

"Was that always the case?" Hendricks asked. "Mia was a year behind us in high school, and you two ran with different groups as I recall."

Jenna cleared her throat repeatedly as if trying to dislodge something, then hacked up and spat out a huge wad of slimy yellow mucus. "Yeah, we didn't really know each other that well until we worked together at the Rummery," she croaked as she flicked her cigarette butt into the yard. "That place looks all nice and shiny on the outside, but working there is like working in a war zone. The staff has to stick together no matter what."

Tom McCarthy: colossal douchebag and abusive boss. A real two-for-one. I couldn't imagine what woman would want to stay married to someone like that. *I wonder what's in it for the wife,* I thought. Then I said: "Tom McCarthy confirmed that he had an affair with Mia. Were you aware of that?"

"Hell yes, I was aware," Jenna said around the fresh cigarette stuck firmly between her teeth. "I remember clear as day the morning she called me up and told me she'd slept with Tom. They'd closed up the Rummery on Saturday night, stayed after everyone else left and had a few drinks, and then she took him home. That was Memorial Day weekend, two thousand nine. Mia was supposed to come over for a barbecue with a bunch of our friends on Sunday afternoon, but she never made it. She was too hung over."

Canceling plans because too much alcohol made her sick? I related a little too hard to that, and I shifted my balance uncomfortably.

"It caused all kinds of problems at work, is what it did." Jenna lit the cancer-stick and took a deep drag.

"Problems?" Hendricks piped in.

"Well, who do you think is going to get the best shifts, the best tables, and a bigger share of the tips?" Jenna pointed her cigarette at Hendricks, and then at me. "The one who's fucking the boss, that's who." Another drag. "That bullshit went on for like four months. Everyone in the back of the house quit because Mia got most of their tips."

"And then the affair ended," I said.

Jenna nodded. "It ended like a nuclear war."

"Tom mentioned it didn't end well," Hendricks said.

"You know why? Because Tom McCarthy is a grade-A chickenshit. Promised her the world, made her fall in love with him, then got cold feet and sent her a breakup text."

I made a mental note to look for that text once we received the log from her carrier.

"I swear she cried for a week straight. Followed Tom around like a pathetic little duckling, begging him to take her back." Jenna shook her head, dropped her cigarette at her feet, and ground it out with her plastic-soled slipper. "Pretty soon he had the restaurant manager schedule her for shifts when he wouldn't be there. Which usually meant closing."

"Did you see Tom McCarthy the day Mia went missing?"

"Actually, yeah. We were short staffed with Mia gone after she had her baby, so he called me to help him unload the truck that morning. It was stupid early, like six-thirty or seven."

That tracked with McCarthy's story, and given Jenna's opinion of her former boss, I thought it likely they were both being truthful.

Hendricks made a note.

After a long pause, during which Jenna stared thoughtfully at a giant fly-encrusted heap of dog dung, she said, "Mia started partying a lot more after Tom dumped her. Went to the bars on Hughes Street after work, and sometimes she came to work still pretty drunk. It was like she was trying to erase the pain with booze." Another pause. "And she was a lot less picky about who she slept with."

Hendricks' eyebrows shot up. "Who else was there?" he asked.

Jenna inhaled deeply, triggering a coughing fit. She regained her composure and rasped, "Ah, let's see. She fucked Alex. Several times, as I recall."

Hendricks and I exchanged a meaningful glance. Alex Blackett had neglected to mention this little detail the other day. I wrinkled my nose at the thought of any woman being intimate with that greasy creep. For such a pretty girl, Mia's taste in men left a lot to be desired.

"Any idea when that was?" Hendricks asked.

"November-December timeframe," Jenna said. "Right around the holidays."

"2009?" I asked.

Jenna nodded. "Yep."

I threw Hendricks another charged look. If what Jenna said was true, it was not outside the realm of possibility that Alex Blackett was Isabel's father.

Hendricks gave an almost imperceptible nod and jotted in his notebook.

I wasn't remotely prepared for what Jenna had to say next. "I believe she also hooked up with Nicholas during that time."

I stared at her dumbly, not sure I'd heard her correctly.

"Nicholas…Faust?" Hendricks asked.

Something was happening to my body. It was spinning. I was floating. My stomach had lodged itself firmly in my throat.

"Yeah. They dated in high school, remember?"

Every cell in my body was spontaneously combusting, but I had to keep my cool. *Straight face, O'Rourke.* Neither Hendricks nor Jenna seemed to notice anything amiss.

"That's right, I do remember them dating in high school," Hendricks said. "They were pretty hot and cold, weren't they?"

"Yeah, it was weird. The most toxic couple I ever saw. They couldn't stand to be together, but they couldn't stand to be apart. And actually, that went on long after high school. On and off. For *years.*"

I was still stuck on *I believe she also hooked up with Nicholas during that time.* He'd never mentioned Mia Masterson's name even once in the time we'd been together. Which was troubling, because from the very beginning of our relationship, we'd promised that we would never lie to each other. Did he never say her name because she was a past lover? Did an omission technically count as a lie? Could Jenna be wrong, maybe thinking of somebody else?

Yes. No. Maybe. I didn't know. God, I wanted to throw up. *You hadn't met him yet. Do you really have any right to be upset?*

My boyfriend had just been linked to a missing woman. Yes, I believed I had every right to be upset. I clasped my hands in front of me to stop them from trembling.

Hendricks asked Jenna Talbot a couple more questions, but I didn't hear any of it. I was too busy thinking about what I would say to Nicholas when I finally got the chance to call him.

He had some explaining to do.

CHAPTER 17

"You're awfully quiet." Hendricks said, shattering my reverie. We were in the car, but I barely remembered saying goodbye to Jenna Spitzer Talbot and leaving her ramshackle house. My consciousness was consumed by thoughts of Nicholas and Mia.

I blinked and looked at him. "Huh?"

"You're a million miles away. Everything all right?"

I had no idea how to answer that, so I didn't bother to try. I just sighed and turned my attention back to the scenery whizzing by outside my car window. *Why didn't he tell me about Mia? Not that I would ever keep score, but I've always been open with him about my past lovers. Why would he hide Mia? What else has he been keeping from me?*

Hendricks tried again. "My finely-honed detective-y senses tell me there's something on your mind." He glanced at me with raised eyebrows. "Want to talk about it?"

I sighed again. "Not really. Sorry."

He stopped trying.

Eventually I realized that the scenery outside looked familiar. There was James Locke outside sweeping his front walk again and keeping a very close eye on Alex Blackett, who was whirring around his yard on an ancient riding lawnmower. "What are we doing back here?"

Hendricks pulled up to the curb in front of Blackett's house, threw the car into park and opened his door. "I have some questions for Alex."

Oh, that's right. Jenna said Mia had been sleeping with Alex. A fact that Alex had conveniently forgotten to mention. I followed.

Blackett saw us coming, shut down his mower, and met us in his driveway. His white t-shirt, this one emblazoned with I MAY BE WRONG BUT IT'S HIGHLY UNLIKELY, was thoroughly soaked and stuck to his skin, and he reeked of hot sunshine and sweat. He looked mildly annoyed to see us. "What can I help you with?"

"Just a couple more questions, Alex," Hendricks said.

"I told you everything I know." Blackett's tone was defiant.

"You and I both know that's not true," Hendricks said. "You sent us to talk to Tom McCarthy, and you know who he said we should talk to? Jenna Spitzer. Remember her?"

Blackett's expression shifted from annoyance to something closer to guilt. "So?"

Hendricks gave an exaggerated sigh. "So, she told us you and Mia had more than just a landlord/tenant relationship. Gotta be honest, Alex, I would much rather have heard that from you when we were here the other day."

Blackett's sweaty face turned a fascinating shade of pink.

"You know how this makes you look, right?" Hendricks asked.

A quick glance across the street confirmed that James Locke was not only still outside his house, but had moved closer and was now sweeping the street gutter. I was sure he could hear every word.

Blackett held his hands up at shoulder level. "Hey, man, I didn't do anything to Mia."

"Except possibly impregnate her," I pointed out.

The look he gave me suggested he wouldn't be sorry to see me burst into flame where I stood.

"I'm still a little fuzzy on why you didn't mention that you'd been sleeping with her, Alex." Hendricks' tone was decidedly frosty.

"I didn't think it mattered," Blackett said. "She disappeared *months* after we stopped fucking."

"From an investigator's perspective, an undisclosed sexual relationship often leads to a motive for murder. Especially when there's a baby with an unknown father." Hendricks was bluffing; we had zero evidence of a murder. But his words seemed to have the desired effect on Alex Blackett.

"No way, man. No *way*. Mia and me were on good terms. Why in the hell would I hurt her?"

I believed him, and Hendricks did too. "All right. If there's anything else we need to know, I suggest you tell us now. Because if I have to come back here again, our next conversation will be in my interrogation room. You don't want that. Trust me. The coffee we serve in there is terrible."

I tried to suppress a smirk – and then it died on my face with Alex's next words.

"I wasn't the only action Mia was getting at the end of two thousand nine. She was fucking Nicholas Faust too. I broke it off with her when I found out. We weren't in a relationship or anything, but I prefer to be the only one buttering a biscuit, if you know what I mean."

"Come on, man." Hendricks rolled his eyes.

A speeding train had run me down for the second time in the space of an hour. Alex Blackett had just destroyed any hope that Jenna had been wrong about Nicholas and Mia. My knees buckled and I sat hard on the curb.

Hendricks dropped to his knees next to me. "Jesus, Raegan, are you okay?"

"I'll grab you a glass of water," Alex said, and turned toward his house. It was a simple gesture, but one that changed how I saw Alex Blackett: deep under the greasy hair, stupid t-shirts, and asshole façade lived a guy who was actually kind of decent. This must have been the Alex that Mia knew.

"No...no, I'm okay. I'm fine." I slowly got to my feet. Hendricks moved with me, his hands hovering just above each of my upper arms so he could grab me if I collapsed again.

"Are you sure?" he asked. His eyes were clouded with concern.

I broke his gaze and brushed off the seat of my shorts. "Yes."

Hendricks turned his attention back to Alex. "When did you say you ended things with Mia?"

"Ah, I didn't. I don't remember the exact day, but I know it was not too long before Christmas."

Hendricks pulled his notebook out of his pocket, flipped to a new page, and jotted this down. "Anything else?"

Blackett shook his head. "That's it, man. I swear."

"All right."

Blackett went back to his mower. Hendricks and I got in the car and headed back to the station.

James Locke declared the gutter in front of his house as clean as it was going to get, and went inside.

∞

At the station, Hendricks headed for the war room and I veered into the empty office across the hall. "I'm sorry, I have to make a phone call first."

His eyes lingered on me for a couple beats. "Okay."

I left him standing in the hallway and closed the door behind me, then sat in the rolling chair behind the bare desk and pulled my cellphone from my purse. My fingers trembled as I called up Nicholas' number. I stared at the photo I had associated with his contact information – a recent selfie he had taken while at work and texted to me. He was dapper in his gray button-down collared shirt, and he had a playful grin on his face. I traced his face with a hovering finger, struck by how it had changed over the years. All youthfulness was gone now, replaced by deepening lines around his eyes and mouth and across his forehead. His black hair and whiskers were threaded with silver. My heart ached. This was the love of my life, the man I'd waited eleven years for – and things between us had been teetering on the brink since his father and grandfather abducted my dad.

And now Mia.

I wasn't sure my heart could take much more torment from Nicholas, but I had to know. I *had* to. So I took a deep breath, steeled my resolve, and touched the green call button.

"Hey babe." Nicholas' strong, smooth voice sounded pleased to hear from me.

"Hey." My heart pounded. "Listen, I –"

"Hold on, let me say something first."

"Okay," I said.

"I shouldn't have shown up at your dad's house in the middle of the night like that. I don't know what I was thinking. Forgive me?"

My eyes burned, and I sighed. "It's fine. There's something else I need to ask you."

"Shoot."

I gritted my teeth and took the plunge. "I just got off the phone with Todd Waterman," I lied. Nicholas didn't know yet that I'd quit the newspaper, a fact that I intended to take full advantage of to get answers about Mia. "He heard from a source at the Minneapolis Police Department that one of their investigators has been looped in on a missing persons case out of River Junction."

"Okay."

"The missing person is a woman named Mia Masterson. I thought you might know her."

Nicholas didn't say anything for so long that I looked at my phone to see if it had dropped the call.

"Nicholas? Still there?"

"Yeah. Yep, still here. Sorry about that. Dropped my phone." His voice had taken on an almost imperceptible edge. "Ah, yes. I knew Mia."

"You did?"

"We went to high school together. Even dated for a while back then."

"Oh, wow." I feigned surprise. "I don't think you've ever mentioned her."

"It was a long time ago, Raegan. We were just kids. We broke up when I left River Junction right after graduation. I never saw her again after that."

I closed my eyes and let my head drop. Tears effervesced behind my eyes. *What else has he been lying to me about all these years?* "Okay."

"I didn't have anything to do with her disappearance, if that's what you're really asking." Nicholas' tone was icy.

"Not at all," I said, pressing my gloved fingertips against my eyelids. "The paper hasn't picked up the story. I was just curious if you knew her, since you and she are both from River Junction. That's all."

A moment of silence, then: "All right. Listen, I gotta go. I'll call you later." And he was gone.

I sat in the abandoned office for a long time, head in my hands, eyes closed, taking deep steady breaths to stave off a rising panic attack. The deteriorating filament holding Nicholas and me together had just snapped. My relationship – my biggest secret and greatest joy for over a decade of my life – was over. I knew it, and I thought he knew it too.

My strength crumbled and great, heaving sobs overcame me. The grief was like swimming against a tidal wave; I couldn't stop it, and it just might drown me. So I clamped my arm over my mouth to muffle the wails bubbling up from deep within me and simply surrendered.

Twenty minutes later I was sweaty and so completely spent that I felt like I could go home, crawl into bed, and sleep for days. I wiped my face with my shirt and waited a few more minutes for some of the redness to fade from my face and eyeballs. I did not want Hendricks to see me like this.

Eventually I felt confident enough to stick my head out into the hallway, look both ways to make sure the coast was clear, and sneak to the ladies' room without anyone seeing me. One look in the mirror confirmed my suspicions: my face was a puffy, blotchy mess. I splashed cold water on it and gazed at my reflection, allowing droplets to fall freely back into the sink. I didn't just look tired; I looked *ragged*. My pale blue eyes were slightly sunken and ringed with dark fatigue, like a raccoon. My cheekbones seemed a little more prominent; had I been eating enough? I thought maybe I hadn't. My fire-red hair, pulled back into a long, curly ponytail at the base of my skull, appeared duller.

It was hard to take proper care of myself when I was suddenly self-employed, I hadn't seen my mother in over three decades, my family was being stalked by a bunch of psychopaths, everyone was keeping secrets from each other, and my relationship was imploding. I sighed and splashed water on my face again, then blotted it with paper towels. I thought I looked put-together enough to finally face Hendricks.

He was probably wondering what had happened to me.

CHAPTER 18

I walked into the war room to find it abandoned. The boxes, the whiteboard, the papers, everything was exactly as we'd left it yesterday. How long had it been since I left him in the hallway?

Long enough for him to disappear, it seemed.

I poked my head into Captain Bailey's office, thinking Hendricks might be in there. Empty. I frowned and made my way to the front desk. Officer Solomon was there, staring at her computer screen in deep concentration.

"Hey," I said, realizing with mild horror that I had no idea what her first name was.

She looked at me and blinked a couple times to refocus her widely-spaced brown eyes. "Oh, hi Raegan. How are you?"

"Fine," I lied. "Have you seen Hendricks?"

She shook her head. "No, I haven't seen Jesse at all yet today."

Huh. "Where did he go?" I wondered out loud.

"Did he take a car?" Solomon asked helpfully.

I snapped my fingers and pointed at her. "I'll go check. Thanks."

Hendricks' name was not on the log, so he hadn't left in a department vehicle. I peeked outside the back door anyway; the fenced parking lot was also deserted.

I give up. I decided to mix business with pleasure and swing in at the Majestic Saloon for a drink. I reasoned that someone there might have worked with Mia back in the day – and besides, I really needed a drink after that disaster of a conversation with Nicholas. Hell, I needed several.

The heat of the day was waning into a mild evening, so I decided to walk the five or six blocks to the Majestic Saloon. Greenhaven Road was quiet, but Hughes Street was bustling with shoppers and folks out for dinner. The Rummery's patio was packed, and several small groups of people milled about on the sidewalk out front waiting to be called to their table.

I thought about Mia as I walked. I searched deep and couldn't find any animosity toward her. She may have been Nicholas' lover, but that was before I met him. I didn't know why Nicholas felt he needed to lie to me about her, but by doing so he'd ignited an ember of doubt deep in my gut. I didn't want to think he could have had anything to do with her disappearance…but like it or not, he was a Faust. And he'd *lied* to me.

The Majestic Saloon was housed in the main floor of a late nineteenth century brick two-story building. Hendricks had said that the Majestic was the oldest bar in River Junction, and it still had much of its original interior. An ornate wood bar ran the length of the main room. The wide wood plank floors were grooved and pitted with wear. Intricately patterned tin tiles covered the ceiling. The lights were dimmed, and the ambience of the barroom made me think that Wyatt Earp should be sitting at a corner table playing poker.

The Majestic was the kind of place where serious drinkers spent their time. There was no kitchen, only copious amounts of peanuts and popcorn, most of which ended up on the floor. Four or five barstools and about half of the small tables were occupied – one of them by Jesse Hendricks. Surprised, I stopped; he appeared to be a finger deep into a glass of whiskey, and stuck way inside his own head.

I wasn't sure I should disturb him. But then his eyes landed on me; he raised the glass in his right hand and gestured to a chair at his table with his left.

I went over and sat. "Hey. I was wondering where you wandered off to."

Hendricks sipped his drink. "Yeah, well, I was wondering when you were going to come out of that office."

He was two or three fingers in on the whiskey, it seemed. "I'm sorry," I said simply. "I had to make an important phone call and lost track of the time."

"More important than finding Mia?" He downed the rest of his drink and signaled the bartender for another one.

I frowned. "It was personal."

"Ah."

Apprehension pierced my heart. "Are you angry with me, Jesse?"

Hendricks looked at me, his eyes dark and wounded, then shook his head and looked away. His drink arrived and he immediately raised the glass to his lips.

I caught the bartender and asked for a glass of chardonnay. He nodded and walked away. I turned back to Hendricks. "Seriously, what is it?"

"I'm not stupid, Raegan. You went all quiet when Jenna mentioned Nicholas Faust's name, and then you almost fainted when Alex did too. As soon as we got back to the station you had to make a personal phone call that took over an hour. I don't need to be a detective to figure out who you were calling."

Fire raced up my neck and into my cheeks. The bartender chose that moment to arrive with my wine. *Thank god.* I took a healthy gulp.

"Here's the deal." Hendricks' voice was completely no-nonsense; he sounded exactly like he had when I first met him at the Ainsley Mansion. "Nicholas Faust's name has now come up twice in this investigation. If you're somehow involved with him, you have to tell me. If you want to keep working this case." A mirthless bark of a laugh escaped him. "Wouldn't that be something? You, an Ainsley, involved with a fucking *Faust?*"

My heart exploded into a panicked gallop in my chest. I opened my mouth to speak, but I couldn't make my tongue form words.

Hendricks stared at me, his eyes round with shock. "You are. You fucking *are*, aren't you?" He ran his hands over his face. "Oh, man, fuck me."

I didn't know I was going to speak until words started tumbling out of my mouth. "No. No, no, Jesse, it's not what you think."

"Oh? What is it, then?

"Well, okay, it is what you think."

"Of course it is," Hendricks muttered. His eyes were dark again.

"Look. Yes. Nicholas and I have been carrying on a secret relationship for a long, long time. But I swear to you, he has never mentioned Mia's name to me." The rest of my wine went down my gullet in a single swallow. "In fact, when I called just now and asked him about her —" I saw the alarm on Hendricks' face and hurriedly added, "Don't worry, I did not tell him I'm helping investigate her disappearance. He doesn't even know yet that I quit the newspaper. As far as he's concerned, I only know about Mia because my editor supposedly has a source at MPD."

Hendricks took a breath. "What did he say?"

"He said he hadn't seen her since high school graduation."

Hendricks raised his eyebrows.

"Right. Exactly. He lied to me." A glass of wine magically appeared in front of me, and I drank. A warm, soft, fuzzy blanket smothered my anger and anxiety.

Hendricks drank, gazing at me over his glass with knitted brows, then asked, "Why?"

I pretended not to know what he was asking. "Why what?"

"Why would you take up with a Faust?"

I shrugged. "He wasn't like his grandfather. Or his father. He was kind, and he loved me, and he may be the only person outside of my family who truly understands my situation."

"Did you worry he would talk to Edison about you?"

"Honestly, no. He never gave me a reason to worry. Until very recently." Glass number two, emptied. The bartender was back with a fresh one within seconds.

"Meaning?" The bartender had brought Hendricks a fresh whiskey too. He'd be getting a fat tip.

"Meaning, since Edison and Morgan abducted my dad, I find that maybe I don't trust Nicholas so much anymore."

Hendricks nodded slowly as he sipped.

"Lying to me was the last straw," I said. "I think – I think he and I are done." It was scary to say those words out loud, and to have someone else hear them. I thought that meant they must be true.

"Does he know that yet?"

"No." Another sip. "Although he knows something's up."

I told Hendricks about Nicholas' surprise visit to my dad's house the night before, and the disastrous phone call on Tuesday night. I even admitted to drinking way too much and ending up with a massive hangover on Wednesday morning. Once again I found myself telling Hendricks way more than I'd intended to. *This guy*, I thought.

"Yeah, that was obvious." Hendricks threw back the rest of his whiskey.

I tried to suppress a smile and failed. "Like any good alcoholic, I prefer to believe I'm awesome at hiding it."

"You're not." His face was emotionless, but I thought I saw the beginnings of a spark in his eyes. *That's better*, I thought. The wounded look they'd had earlier hurt my heart.

"I'm really sorry, Jesse," I said. "I should have told you about Nicholas as soon as his name came up."

Hendricks sat up and leaned on his elbows over the small round table between us. I did the same. His face was so close to mine I could smell the whiskey on his breath. *Bourbon*, I thought. "We'll go see Captain Bailey tomorrow, and you'll have to tell her what you just told me."

Panic bubbled in my throat. "But – what if she pulls me off the case?"

"She might," he acknowledged. "But then again, she might not. Either way, no more secrets." He extended his hands in front of him on the table, palms up. "Take off your gloves."

"Why?"

"Just trust me. Please."

This was an odd request, but my curiosity got the best of me. I pulled my gloves off and set them on the edge of the table.

Hendricks closed and reopened his hands, gesturing for me to put my hands in them. The thought of touching his bare skin with mine made my heart skip a beat. I took a deep breath and grasped them, unsure what to expect. His hands closed around mine, enveloping them in warmth and making my entire spine tingle – and something strange happened. I expected to see a vision pop up behind my eyes, but none did; Hendricks' face stayed right in front of me. His lips never moved, but clear as day I heard his voice say *She's amazing. I've never met anyone like her.*

My visions had always been soundless; they were much like watching TV with the volume turned all the way down. So to hear Hendricks' voice in my head startled me, and quite badly. My body jerked and my hands involuntarily clamped on his.

"Whoa," he said. "Raegan?"

"I –" My train of thought was interrupted by his voice again: *I don't know. I'm afraid to ask her.*

I yanked my hands out of his, leaned back in my chair, and crossed my arms over my chest.

Baffled, Hendricks asked, "What? What did you see?"

"I didn't *see* anything," I said. My heart pounded in my throat. *What the hell just happened? Was he talking about me?*

"You didn't have a vision?"

"No, I had a…" I realized I didn't have a word for what I'd just experienced; I learned everything I knew about my touch from Mimi, and her visions had no sound either. "I *heard* something."

Hendricks frowned. "What did you hear?"

I had a slightly more important question for him as I pulled my gloves back on my hands: "What did you expect I would see?"

He sighed. "While you were holed up in the office across the hall, I went and checked in with Captain Bailey. Gave her an update on progress with the case. She was so pleased she actually *smiled*. She never does that. I wanted to surprise you, let you see for yourself. She's very impressed with you, Raegan."

I wondered if the snippets I'd heard were from that conversation. Decided to ask. "What are you afraid to ask me?"

Hendricks stared at me dumbly for a few beats. "What do you mean?"

"Well, one of the things I heard was your voice saying you were 'afraid to ask her.'" I crooked my fingers in air quotes for emphasis.

His face visibly reddened, even in the dimness of the Majestic Saloon's barroom.

I signaled for two more drinks. "You might as well tell me, Jesse. I can just as easily swing by Bailey's office and touch her desk, find out that way."

Cornered, he pushed air out through pursed lips — lips I kind of wanted to kiss. "She asked me if you were married, had a family. I told her I was afraid to ask because by then I had my suspicions about Nicholas Faust. Didn't want her to know anything about that until I had a chance to talk to you." Another whiskey appeared in front of him.

I picked up my new glass of wine and sipped. *Gonna need to slow down if I want to get home tonight.* I suspected it might already be too late for that, and I didn't care; I sort of liked the idea of going home with Jesse Hendricks.

Hendricks drank about half of his whiskey and pushed it away. "I'm done, man." He looked at me with bleary, red-rimmed eyes. "We gotta work tomorrow."

"I know." I gulped the rest of my wine and resisted the urge to order yet another one. *How many is that, anyway?* I'd lost count. I did know that I was in for another tough morning.

"You can't drive." He wasn't asking.

"I know."

"I live six blocks from here. We can walk. I got a pretty comfy couch."

"Okay." Something in my belly ignited.

The walk to his house was quiet, both of us lost in our drunken thoughts. Hendricks stumbled once, nearly falling off the curb and into the street. I grabbed his arm to steady him as best I could, then wrapped my arm around his waist so we could support each other as we walked.

It took us a while to navigate the streets north of downtown River Junction, but eventually we came upon a neat little white stucco Cape Cod with red trim and shutters. "Here we are," he announced, his voice rough. He struggled for a moment to unlock the side door, then finally pushed it open. "Come in."

I followed him inside and found myself in his darkened kitchen. It was quite modern and every bit as neat as the exterior of the home. He led me into the living room, switched on a brass table lamp, and gestured toward a comfortable-looking sofa the color of oatmeal. "Ah, so there it is. I'll go get you a blanket."

Without realizing I was going to do anything, I grabbed his hand and said, "Hold on." I pulled him down and we sat, knees to knees. My head buzzed and my eyes felt heavy. I had no idea what I was going to say until words began falling from my mouth. "I – I just wanted to say thank you, Jesse."

"For what?" He frowned with the effort of focusing his attention on me, and his bloodshot eyes looked as bleary as mine felt.

"For taking me on. I know I can be a pain in the ass."

Hendricks shrugged. "We all have our moments."

I couldn't help myself. I reached out, slid my gloved hand behind the nape of his neck, and pulled his face to mine. He started to speak, but I hushed him with a deep kiss.

I half expected him to break away in horror, sputtering words about not getting involved with coworkers, but he didn't. He returned the kiss with interest. His lips were warm and moist and tasted like Jack Daniels. He wrapped his arms around my back and pulled my body against his, then gently guided me backward until I was lying on the couch and he was lying on top of me.

Hendricks was bigger in height and weight than Nicholas; the warmth and pressure of his body against mine was comforting. I felt safe. Protected. He let go of my lips and moved to my neck, leaving a tingling trail of butterfly kisses. Snippets of blurry visions popped up with every touch of his hands or lips; I ignored them. My hands explored the topography of his muscular arms, shoulders and back. We were close to the point of no return. I could feel it, and I welcomed it.

That is, until Hendricks cupped my face in his hands and touched my forehead with his. Suddenly all I could see behind my eyes were images – blurry due to the effects of alcohol, but obviously from the horse figurine vision – of Mia Masterson getting it on with Tom McCarthy. My stomach turned. I felt...dirty somehow. I didn't fully understand why, but I was desperate to get Hendricks off me.

"Wait. Stop." I worked my hands between our enmeshed bodies and pushed his chest.

Hendricks did a basic pushup to lift himself up. "What? What's wrong?" he asked, concerned and confused, a little out of breath.

I squirmed out from under him and scooted to the end of the couch, where I tucked my feet under me. "We can't do this."

"Why not?" Hendricks sat next to me.

"It's just – I can't stop thinking about Mia."

Hendricks surprised me by nodding soberly. "Cases have a way of getting in your blood." He stood, adjusted the crotch of his pants, and headed toward the back of the house. "Let me grab you that blanket."

I took it gratefully, curled up on the impossibly comfortable sofa, and buried myself underneath it. Despite the persistent alcohol buzz in my head, I was unconscious in seconds.

Friday, July 16, 2021

CHAPTER 19

I regained consciousness before the sun rose, feeling like I'd been hit by a Mack truck. I hadn't gotten a wink of actual sleep, my mouth tasted like death, and my whole head was stuck in a steadily tightening vise. I groaned. *God, why do I do this to myself?*

Hendricks' house was quiet. I dug my phone out of my purse and checked the time: 5:15. I noticed two text messages waiting for me: one from my dad, who wondered when I might be home, and one from Nicholas. I didn't read that one.

I replied to my dad and then sent Hendricks a quick text: Heading home to clean up, see you at the station. I folded the blanket and laid it neatly over the arm of the couch, tiptoed back through the kitchen, and let myself out the back door. The pre-dawn air was muggy and mild, and the eastern horizon was a brilliant shade of pink.

The maps app on my phone guided me back to my car along quiet neighborhood streets. Hendricks lived in an area of River Junction that had been built to house returning World War II veterans and their growing families. All of the houses looked just like his, some with minor differences like dormer windows, fireplaces, and breezeways.

I thought about Hendricks as I walked. The wounded look in his eyes when I first arrived at the bar. His strong yet gentle hands. The feel of his weight against my body. Gentle kisses on my neck. Things had changed dramatically between us; would it be awkward now? Did I have any regrets? Did I feel bad for nearly cheating on Nicholas? I dug deep, looked in every crevice of my soul, and decided: No. I had no regrets.

Nicholas and I were done. And I thought there was potential for something great with Hendricks. If, that was, he felt the same way. I thought maybe he did.

Soon I found myself back downtown, walking along Greenhaven Road. My car was right where I'd left it, in the parking lot outside the police station.

Two hours later my car was back in the same spot. I walked into the war room showered, hydrated, medicated, caffeinated, and feeling more like an actual human being. Hendricks was already there, dressed in khakis and a black polo shirt, and he looked as rumpled and out of sorts as I felt. He was deep in concentration, poring over a thick stack of papers.

"Hey." I braced myself for the awkwardness.

To Hendricks' credit, and much to my relief, there was none. He looked up from his papers, the skin around his drawn eyes much darker than usual, and smiled. "Good morning. Your coffee is right over there."

"Ah. Thank you." I inhaled bitter vapors, then drank. It tasted like the nectar of the gods. *What is it about Beananza's coffee that makes it so damn good?* I wondered. "What do you have there?"

He gestured at the stack. "Mia's text records finally came through last night."

"About damn time," I said, and sat across the desk from him. I couldn't wait to dig in and look for clues.

Hendricks peeled half of the papers from the top of the stack and handed them to me. "You take a look at these, I'll take the rest. You want the pink highlighter, or the green one?"

The sparkle in his eyes made me chuckle. I found myself wishing I hadn't chickened out on him last night. "Ah, pink I guess. Did you check who she sent her last text to before she disappeared?"

"Yeah. It's a number I don't recognize. It's not associated with anyone on the board." he flipped through pages until he found what he was looking for.

I frowned and held my gloved hand out. "Let me see."

Hendricks handed me a single sheet of paper, and I eagerly read Mia's final text conversation.

DATE	TIME	FROM_USER	TO_USER	MESSAGE
21-Sep-2010	23:15:42	7634145233	9526335987	I brought your daughter home yesterday. You should come by and meet her.
21-Sep-2010	23:20:02	9526335987	7634145233	That's not my fucking daughter. Stop saying it is.
21-Sep-2010	23:28:44	7634145233	9526335987	She's so beautiful.
21-Sep-2010	23:30:11	7634145233	9526335987	She looks just like you.
21-Sep-2010	23:35:34	9526335987	7634145233	The kid probably has ten fathers, the way your whore ass slept around town.
21-Sep-2010	23:37:04	9526335987	7634145233	If it's money you're after, go get it from Blackett and leave me alone.
21-Sep-2010	23:48:10	7634145233	9526335987	He's not the father. You are.

21-Sep-2010	23:52:22	9526335987	7634145233	Fuck that. If you tell even one person that's my kid, I'll fucking kill you and make the kid an orphan. Nobody will ever find you. Do you understand me?
21-Sep-2010	23:48:10	7634145233	9526335987	Your loss.

Chills ran the length of my spine, making me shiver in spite of the warm coffee in my hand. "Mia disappeared less than eight hours after she sent that last text. Which was in response to a direct threat."

"Whoever that phone number belongs to just shot to the top of our suspect list."

I brought the paper up to my face and squinted at the phone numbers. Hendricks had written "Mia" next to the number with the 763 area code. The other one, though…

Like most people, I didn't bother memorizing phone numbers anymore; I just loaded names and numbers into the contacts list on my phone and watched the caller ID magic happen when someone called me. But something about the unidentified 952 number seemed…

My heart stuttered. "Oh, no." I reached for my purse. "Oh, no no no."

"What is it?" Hendricks asked.

I pulled my phone out and called up my text messages. The unread message from Nicholas sat at the top of the list. I tapped to open it and there, right there, was his number: (952) 633-5987. My erratic heart fell into the deep pit that had opened in my gut.

"Son of a bitch!" I hissed through clenched teeth. Tears pulsed behind my eyes.

Hendricks held out his hand. "Let me see."

I gave him my phone and covered my face with my gloved hands. I didn't want him to see me cry.

"Holy shit," Hendricks breathed. Then: "Raegan."

I shook my head wildly, still hiding my tears.

His hand, warm and strong, took my wrist. "Raegan. Look at me."

A huge, watery sob escaped me, and I lowered my hands.

He seemed utterly unperturbed by the condition of my face. "Two things. We have to talk to Captain Bailey ASAP. And, did you read this text message?"

I shook my head. I didn't dare open my mouth.

"It says 'Call me. We need to talk.' Sent after midnight last night."

I'd been actively avoiding having any sort of meaningful discussion with Nicholas. I squeezed my eyes shut against another wave of tears.

Hendricks stood and stepped around the desk, holding his arms out in front of him. "Come here."

I went to him, buried my face in his chest, and disintegrated. He wrapped his arms protectively around me and let me cry, but only for a minute or two.

"All right, come on. Pull yourself together now."

I took a couple of deep breaths, my face still buried in his black polo shirt. His personal scent reminded me of the color blue and helped calm me. "Okay."

He moved his hands to my upper arms and gently pushed me away from him so he could look me in the eye. "You going to be all right?"

"I don't know," I admitted, wiping my face with the hem of my shirt.

"Look, I can only imagine how much this sucks for you, Raegan. But you have to control your emotions if you want to keep working this case."

"I know. I know."

"Come on, let's go see if Bailey's in her office."

My heart sank, but I obliged. "All right."

I followed him.

∞

"Well." Sarah Bailey's face was carefully neutral, but her almond eyes snapped. "You've gotten yourselves into a situation, haven't you?"

"Not intentionally, Captain," Hendricks said. "It's not like we knew Nicholas Faust would end up as a suspect in Mia's disappearance."

Bailey's eyes slid to me. "What I don't understand is, why you didn't disclose from the very beginning that you were involved with a Faust. That would have been pertinent information regardless, and likely would have affected my decision to bring you on."

My face burned, but I maintained eye contact. "I didn't think it mattered. And I've told literally nobody, ever, until Jesse asked me about it yesterday."

"Hm." She didn't look convinced, and if I were being honest, my excuses sounded lame to my own ears. I'd fucked up, and I knew it.

"I'm sorry," I said.

Bailey gave me a long, measured look. "Ms. O'Rourke, I should end your consultancy right now. But I have a problem. You and Officer Hendricks have made more progress on this case in five days than anyone in this department has managed in eleven years. I'm more confident every day that this case will be solved. The chief is too. Hell, the whole *community* is eagerly watching and waiting to finally learn what happened to Mia Masterson. I would be a damn fool to stop your momentum now. So I'm willing to give you another chance."

Relief washed over me, and I exhaled air I didn't realize I'd been holding. "Tha—"

"With conditions."

"Okay."

Bailey's eyes burned. "You are not, under any circumstances, to communicate with Nicholas Faust. At all. He is officially a suspect in Mia's disappearance, and to do so would seriously jeopardize this investigation. Am I making myself clear?"

"Perfectly," I said. My heart fluttered.

"I was able to talk the county attorney out of pressing charges for attempted assault and discharging a firearm. I don't think I could do it again for obstruction of justice."

I didn't have any problem catching her meaning: *Tell Nicholas he's a suspect and you will go to prison.* "Yes, ma'am."

"Officer Hendricks will be responsible for all communication with and about Nicholas Faust, in his capacity as a licensed law enforcement officer. Run this investigation exactly by the book. Do you understand?"

"Yes," Hendricks and I said in unison.

Bailey's eyes softened. "You're so close. Don't disappoint me, Raegan."

That hurt more than the threats. Way more. "I'm sorry, Captain. I won't."

"Okay, then. Go find Mia."

We went.

CHAPTER 20

We filed back into the war room and took our respective seats. Hendricks propped his elbows on his chair's armrest, tented his fingers in front of his face, and gazed at me. "So how is it that an Ainsley ended up falling in love with a Faust, anyway?"

I didn't love his tone, but it was a fair question. "We met at a charity masquerade ball at the Harper Pax Art Center. I was there with my editor, covering for a colleague who was out on maternity leave. Nicholas was there specifically to kill me."

Hendricks blinked. "Clearly he didn't succeed."

"No. I felt him coming and confronted him. Took him by surprise. We recognized each other immediately.

"We were surprised by each other. Fascinated. We didn't feel the hate that our families always told us we should. Instead we talked. Got to know one another. He wasn't the monster I'd always been told all Fausts are. He was kind, and gentle, and he loved me. He risked his life to love me." I sighed. "Our relationship is basically text messages, phone calls, and occasional visits to his place or mine. It's not a super solid foundation for a relationship, but I'll tell you what – I was prepared to wait for him for the rest of my life, if that's what it took. I put my entire life on hold for him."

Hendricks thought about this for a moment. "I find it hard to believe that he never tried to pump you for information about your mom."

"He hated his grandfather and everything he stands for. He promised to do everything in his power to protect me and my family. We didn't hear from Edison or Morgan Faust for a lot of years because Nicholas was sabotaging Edison's plans behind the scenes."

"But then they kidnapped your dad."

"Yes."

"What do you think changed?"

I shrugged. "I don't know, but obviously *something* has. I do wonder if Edison has become a much stronger influence on Nicholas." I remembered how he showed up unannounced at my dad's house in the middle of the night, expecting to be let in as if he belonged there, and shivered.

Hendricks nodded as I talked, taking it all in. "When did you say you first met Nicholas?"

"I don't think I did say. October thirtieth, two thousand ten."

Hendricks was silent for a few beats, studying his hands. His next words were slow and deliberate. "That – ah, that was a little more than a month after Mia went missing."

My insides seized like gears in a rusty old clock. My stomach rolled, and everything I'd consumed that day made its way back up my esophagus.

"Excuse me," I croaked and ran for the restroom, hand clamped over my mouth. I barely made it over the toilet in time. My stomach heaved up coffee and hot brown bile until there was nothing left but air bubbles – and kept on heaving. For one miserable, sweaty minute I thought I might actually puke my guts out.

Finally the dry heaves subsided. I flushed the mess away and sat against the cool tile wall, panting, waiting for my heart to slow and the sweat to evaporate.

A soft knock on the door and Hendricks' muffled voice. "Raegan? Are you all right?"

No crying, O'Rourke. "I'll be out in a second, okay?"

"Okay."

I took another minute or two to collect myself, then stood up, washed my hands and face, and rinsed my mouth out. *I hope I have mints in my purse.*

Hendricks watched me walk back into the war room, his face creased with worry. "You sure you're okay?"

I was suddenly very tired of hearing that question, and I couldn't keep the irritation out of my voice. "Honestly, no. I'm not okay."

"Maybe you should step back from this case, Raegan. For your own well-being. I'm worried about you."

I thought about Mia's text messages to Nicholas: *She's so beautiful.* Those were the words of a new mother in love with her child. Words full of wonder and hope for the future. Whatever had happened to her and Isabel, they didn't deserve it. The injustice burned within me like an ember. I had to find her. I had to know. Even if it was Nicholas who hurt her or caused her disappearance.

"No. I'm staying on. Just do me a favor and please stop asking me if I'm okay."

Hendricks blinked.

"Despite my previously-unknown personal connections to this case, it's not about me. It's about Mia and Isabel. I'm giving it everything I have while my entire life changes around me. I'm not okay now, but I will be. Eventually. All right?"

"All right. But do me one favor."

I sighed. Exhaustion enveloped me like a dust storm. "What's that?"

"Go home. Get some rest. Neither of us got much sleep last night."

I was mildly shocked at his mention of the previous night's activities. "About that," I began.

Hendricks held up a hand. "I want to apologize. I was drunk and got caught up in the moment, and it was inappropriate. It shouldn't have happened."

My heart deflated like a balloon. I'd thought maybe he'd felt something building between us like I did, but it seemed I was mistaken. Another layer of sad added to my ever-building sadness parfait.

"We're colleagues working on a case together, and you have a super complex situation to navigate, and I don't need to be making things worse. I'm sorry, Raegan."

"I'm not," I said. Surprise subtly changed the contours of his face. And was that a tinge of regret in his eyes for dismissing what had happened between us so quickly? I hoped so. I lifted my purse from the desk and slung it over my shoulder. "I'm going to take you up on your offer. I'll see you in the morning, okay?"

"Tomorrow's Saturday."

"I know," I lied. The truth was, all of my days started running together after I quit the newspaper. The absence of the daily routine made it damn near impossible for me to keep my days straight. "I'm planning to come in. There's still all those texts to look through."

Hendricks pondered this. "Maybe I'll join you."

"Cool," I said, and headed for home.

My bed was calling my name.

∞

I arrived at my dad's house to find Mimi and Kieran sitting in the living room, watching Mimi's favorite soap opera on TV. They turned in tandem to look at me when I walked in, and they both frowned. *I must look like a complete disaster,* I thought.

Mimi patted the couch cushion next to her. "Come and sit down, love."

I trudged over and sat.

"You look like shit," Kieran observed.

"Thanks," I said.

"Is it this case you're working on?" he asked. "What happened?"

"Want to talk about it?" Mimi chimed in.

I gave a long, deep sigh. I wouldn't be able to tell Mimi and Kieran the latest about Mia's case without mentioning Nicholas. It seemed the time had come to confess my secret. *It's over anyway,* I thought, resigned. "There's something I need to tell you guys." I scanned the room. "Where's Dad?"

"Out," Mimi said.

I was too deep in my own head to really notice her abrupt answer or ask for clarification. Eleven years was a long time to keep a secret from my family. Secrets are corrosive, and mine had been eating through my conscience. It was finally time to come clean.

"Please be kind," I said. And I told them everything.

Mimi and Kieran sat and listened without interrupting me. It was like they sensed my burden was too heavy, and if I stopped I might never start again.

Half an hour and a box of tissues later, the television had changed over from soaps to talk shows and I felt better. Lighter. We all sat in silence for a moment; a frown etched Kieran's forehead and Mimi's eyes were wide with shock. I braced myself for the backlash.

That wasn't what I got. "Oh, honey." Mimi rubbed my shoulder. "This is a terrible burden to carry all by yourself. Why didn't you say anything sooner?"

Tears overflowed again. I picked up the tissue box, realized it was empty, tossed it on the coffee table, and wiped my face with my t-shirt. "B-b-because I thought you'd be so mad at me for getting involved with a F-f-faust." A shaky sob escaped me. "I couldn't stand the thought of disappointing you. Or anyone."

Kieran, chin lowered, looked at me from under his eyebrows. "Before Dad was taken, we hadn't heard much of the Fausts in a long time. Do you think Nicholas had something to do with that?"

I nodded. "I know he did."

Kieran turned his attention to Mimi. "Nicholas Faust must not be *all* bad, Mimi."

Mimi shook her head. "As Fausts go, no. I always thought he had the most potential for good of any of them. Thanks to his mother, Laura. She was a childhood friend of Danielle's. A lovely girl." Mimi sighed. "Morgan had some trouble with women, as I understand. So his father chose one for him."

"What kind of trouble?" I asked, fascinated. *Shy? Awkward? Gay?* Nicholas had told me about his mother, but I'd never heard the backstory around how and why she'd ended up with Morgan Faust. I'd always wondered.

Mimi shrugged. "I don't know, but somehow Edison convinced Laura's parents to marry her off to Morgan. I'm sure he made it difficult for them to refuse."

"You mean, like a bribe or something?" I asked.

"Or maybe extortion," Kieran added.

"Or threats. All are well-used tools in Edison's arsenal." Mimi folded her hands in her lap. "Anyway, Morgan and Laura married in nineteen eighty-one, and Nicholas came along less than a year later. They divorced within two years – Morgan had a nasty habit of beating his wife black and blue – and Laura won physical and legal custody of Nicholas."

"In Greenhaven County?" I asked, remembering something Jesse Hendricks had said the first day I met him: *Edison Faust has an absolute chokehold on this town. Everyone is afraid of him and his son.* It stood to reason that family court judges in River Junction would not be immune to Edison's brand of domestic terror.

Mimi held up a gnarled finger. "Ah! No, Morgan and Laura were living in Minneapolis at the time."

Edison would have had no leverage over officials in Hennepin County, and so was powerless to stop the court from awarding custody of Nicholas to his mother.

"I bet that put a target on Laura's back," I said. I was about to ask how she died, then remembered that Nicholas had told me the night we met: *I'm frankly surprised Edison let her live as long as she did. She passed away ten years ago. Heart attack.* I'd taken him at his word then, but now I suspected it wasn't really a heart attack that killed Laura. After all, Nicholas had been sent to the masquerade ball to kill me with a succinylcholine injection. *The untraceable drug,* I thought.

"Do you think Edison and Morgan influence Nicholas more than they did before?" Kieran asked.

"It's possible," I said. "When we first met he was one hundred percent anti-Edison. He wanted nothing to do with him or Morgan. But..." I sighed. "I suppose when you have the devil whispering in your ear long enough, you eventually start to believe him."

Kieran gave me a frank look. "Do you think he was involved in Dad's abduction?"

A pit opened in my stomach. "He swears he wasn't. But...I honestly don't know if I believe him. Now that I know he lied to me about Mia Masterson, I can't help but think he's lied about other things too." I took a ragged breath.

Kieran pointed at me. "You know what Edison's plan is, don't you? And why he's after Mom again."

"Yes." I told him and Mimi the story of Jack Hughes' gold. "Edison wants to force Mom to touch Jack's things and tell him where to find the gold."

Kieran shook his head. "It'll never work. He'd need just the right object, and too much time has passed."

I glanced at Mimi, and she nodded grimly. "Actually..."

By the time she finished explaining the true depth and breadth of Danielle's touch, Kieran's eyes were the size of dinnerplates.

He too was shocked that Mimi would lie to us about such a fundamental fact about our mother, but he accepted it much more quickly than I expected. His eyes moved to me. "I see now why you changed your mind about bringing Mom home. This...this changes *everything*."

I nodded. "Nicholas says Edison is convinced the gold exists and there's a lot of it. He will do anything to get his hands on it."

Kieran cocked his head, considering. "I think Nicholas is working with Edison on this gold thing."

I rolled my eyes. "You're wrong. Why would he tell me what Edison is planning if he's in on it?"

Kieran shrugged. "I don't know. Maybe he's trying to pump you for information while pretending to be all helpful."

"As far as he's concerned, I still don't know where Mom is. And he has never asked."

"Then maybe he's just trying to have it both ways," Kieran said. "Help his grandpa and still hang on to you. Whatever it is, he's dirty."

I shook my head and chuckled. "When did you become a conspiracy theorist, Kieran?"

"Since I found out you've been dating a Faust for the past *decade*, Raegan." His derisive tone matched mine.

"I deserve that," I said. "But I don't care what you say, Nicholas would never intentionally hurt me like that. Never."

"All right, you two. That's enough," Mimi interjected. "Your dad said no more fighting, remember?"

I stuck my tongue out at Kieran.

Kieran and Mimi both laughed. Then my brother asked, "What are you going to do?"

"Nothing right now. I can't talk to Nicholas at all," I said. "Not until the Mia Masterson case is done. Captain Bailey has told me in no uncertain terms that she will throw my ass in jail if I do."

Kieran's copper eyebrows went up, but he did not ask me to elaborate. "After that?"

"After that, whenever that is, I officially end things with him." It still felt weird to say out loud.

"You be careful, love." Mimi's eyes brimmed with pure anxiety. "Remember that Nicholas is still a Faust."

"He wouldn't hurt me, Mimi. He loves me." A tiny, whispery voice deep in the recesses of my mind asked, *Are you sure?* I shook it off.

"Still. They're all unpredictable and dangerous. Especially when they're angry."

I patted her hands. "I'll be okay, Mimi. I can't do anything right now anyway."

Famous last words.

PART 3:
MIA & ISABEL

Friday, July 17, 2021

CHAPTER 21

Of course my sleep was plagued by dreams of Nicholas; he was on my mind constantly since our last tense conversation. The revelation that he'd lied to me about Mia Masterson had solidified what I already knew but didn't want to acknowledge since my dad's abduction: our relationship was over, the victim of the feud between our families. And the fact that I could do nothing about it as long as I was working Mia's case was really hard. I didn't want to prolong things. I wanted to move on with my life. And, if I were being honest with myself, I wanted to explore all the possibilities with Jesse Hendricks – my broken, masochistic, kind and lovable wannabe detective.

Despite the crazy dreams, I awoke sober and fairly refreshed…but restless. I quickly showered, made coffee, and hit the road for River Junction just as the sun was coming up. I wanted to see what else was in Mia's text messages, and I hoped the station would be somewhat quiet so I could concentrate without distractions.

I settled into the war room and stared at the photo of Mia on Hendricks' whiteboard while I sipped my coffee. She held her shotglass up in an eternal toast, a carefree smile on her face. She was beautiful; it wasn't hard to see how she'd captured the affections of Alex Blackett, Tom McCarthy, and Nicholas Faust.

At some point Hendricks had scribbled "32 minutes" in the upper left corner of the whiteboard – and it dawned on me that we hadn't yet established where Mia went after James Locke saw her drive away at 7:45 a.m. the day she disappeared. For god's sake, we had names of people to talk to and we hadn't even followed up with them yet.

Captain Bailey thinks we're making progress on this case? I thought. *It's actually been nothing but distractions.*

I looked up the number for River Drug, hoping to catch Lyle Allister, the pharmacist. I was in luck.

"Oh, sure, just hold on a moment." The woman on the phone had the strongest Canadian accent I'd ever heard. Her O's were longer than the Autobahn.

I had just enough time to grab a notebook and pen before a gruff voice got on the line. "This is Lyle, can I help you?"

"Mr. Allister, my name is Raegan O'Rourke. I'm an investigator assisting the River Junction Police Department with the disappearance of Mia Masterson back in twenty-ten. How are you today?"

"Oh, fine, fine. Yes, I remember Mia. Such a tragedy."

"Mr. Allister, I understand that you saw her the morning she went missing. Can you tell me about that encounter?"

"I spoke with John Baker about this back then, told him everything I know."

"I believe you, sir, but unfortunately I don't have a record of that in the case files. I just need to make sure that we have a complete timeline of Mia's whereabouts leading up to when she and baby Isabel went missing."

"All right," Allister said, sounding doubtful but willing to help. "She was waiting at the door when we opened at eight o'clock. She had the baby with her."

I made a note. "Did she say why she was there so early?"

"She asked about baby formula. She was having trouble nursing and worried that the baby wasn't getting enough to eat." He paused. "The baby was fussing, and a parent will do just about anything to calm a fussy baby. I know, I had four myself, all with colic. My wife is an angel, I'll tell you." Allister chuckled.

I thought of something James Locke had said: *She was kinda hunched over at the waist, like her stomach hurt. Taking slow steps. She seemed to have a hard time carrying the carseat too.* "Did she seem all right to you, Mr. Allister?"

"No, she didn't seem all right at all. You know, I expect a new mother to look tired. But Mia…Mia looked sick."

My pen flew over the paper as I furiously scrawled notes. "Sick how?"

"She did mention she was experiencing some abdominal pain. She asked me to read the labels on the formula cans to her because she couldn't focus her eyes. And her face…her face was rather puffy. All of which she chalked up to recovering from childbirth. She bought two cans of powdered formula and two bottles, and went on her way. That was probably about eight fifteen."

I scribbled all this on my notebook paper. I hoped I'd be able to read my own handwriting later.

"And aside from the fact that she was clearly under the weather, Mia seemed fine? No nervousness or anxiety?"

"No. She just wanted to feed that poor baby."

I thanked him for his time. "You've been really helpful, Mr. Allister."

"I hope you find her, Ms. O'Rourke. This town hasn't quite been the same since she went missing."

What I thought: *And it might be all Nicholas' fault.*

What I said: "I hope so too."

I hung up and went to the whiteboard, where I noted that Mia had gone to River Drug the morning of September 22 to buy formula for her baby and left at about 8:15 a.m. I'd narrowed our timeframe down to just two minutes.

Where did you go, Mia? I thought, gazing at the oversized map of River Junction on the wall. *After the drugstore, where did you go?* I looked up the location of the Junction Medical Clinic and discovered it was on the far south end of town. *Is that where you were headed?*

I was debating whether or not it would be worth calling the clinic to see if I could find someone who remembered Mia calling that morning when my eyes fell upon an oversized yellow envelope sitting on Hendricks' side of the desk. Someone had written **JESSE: FOR YOUR EYES ONLY** in black permanent marker on it, and the printed label read simply FAUST SURVEILLANCE 7/16/21.

"What the fuck is this?" I muttered, snatching the envelope and opening the flap on one end. I supposed it made sense for Hendricks to put the Fausts under surveillance after Nicholas' name came up in the Mia Masterson investigation, but why wouldn't he tell me about it? I ignored a twinge of guilt in my gut as I opened the envelope. *He's going to show me anyway,* I reasoned.

A single printed eight-by-ten photograph slid out onto the desk. I held it up and squinted at it. At first I wasn't sure what I was looking at, but when I finally got it oriented correctly I realized the photo was shot from a distance, zoomed in on a window set in a formidable-looking rough granite wall. I'd never been to the Fortress, but I'd heard enough about the Fausts' family home to recognize it.

On the other side of the window, inside the house, Edison, Morgan, and Nicholas Faust huddled around a computer monitor situated on an ornate wooden desk. The screen faced the window, and the backs of the mens' heads were clearly visible. Nicholas was pointing at something on the screen. I squinted to see the image more clearly – and it rocked my world to its very core.

The image on the Fausts' computer screen was a scan of the deed for Carl Engelman's property in Isabella, Minnesota.

I dropped the photo and covered the lower half of my face with my gloved hands, my eyes wide. Nicholas had lied to me about why he was in River Junction. He didn't come up here on some baseless whim of Edison's. He was using his vast computer skills to help Edison track my mother down – and he'd succeeded.

Edison Faust knew where my mother was.

My heart pounded in my throat, stealing my breath, and my brain lost its grip on all rational thought. Running on pure impulse, not thinking for one second about the consequences, I picked up my cellphone and dialed Nicholas' number.

"Hey babe," he answered jovially.

"Don't you 'hey babe' me," I hissed. "No more fucking *games.*"

197

A moment of silence on the other end of the line. He tried again to maintain his façade. "I don't –"

"Just stop. Stop *lying* to me, Nicholas."

A much longer pause, and when he spoke his tone could have shaved ice. "And what is it, exactly, you think I've lied about?"

"Why are you in River Junction?"

"I told you, Edison summoned me. I really don't know why. He's not one who feels compelled to state his reasons."

"Yeah, see, I know that's a fucking lie. You're there to help him track down my mother. Don't bother lying anymore, I have proof."

More silence from his end; I went ahead and filled it. "I also know that you were a lot closer to Mia Masterson than you let on. She thought you were the father of her baby. And you threatened her the night before she went missing. How do you think that makes you look?"

"I had nothing to do with Mia's disappearance." The rage was perfectly clear in his voice, and its intensity sent chills down my spine.

"I have never lied to you, Nicholas. Not once in eleven years." My throat hurt with the effort of controlling it; I wanted to scream until this whole nightmare ended. "And every single thing that comes out of your mouth lately is a lie. It makes me wonder if you've ever told me the truth about anything."

"You have no idea the things I've done for you and your family, Raegan."

"I know you worked behind the scenes for a long time to protect my family, just like you promised me you'd do. And you know I appreciate it. But then – but then my dad got snatched right out of his fucking driveway. So tell me, Nicholas, what's changed?"

Nicholas didn't answer. Which was all the answer I needed.

"We're done," I said. My heart broke in half inside my chest.

"Raegan —"

"My Mimi was right. At the end of the day you are a Faust, and Fausts can't be trusted. I was a damn fool to believe otherwise."

"You're making a huge mistake."

"Goodbye, Nicholas." I ended the call and tossed my phone in my purse. It immediately began ringing and buzzing. I ignored it and propped my head in my hands, waiting for the tears to come. They didn't. Instead my thoughts shifted to my mother. I had to let my family know that she was in real danger.

"What are you doing?"

I looked up, and there was Hendricks standing in the doorway. He held two coffees from Beananza and his eyes moved between the surveillance photo on the desk, my cellphone in my purse, and my face.

I tried to smile. "Jesus, Jesse, you scared the crap out of me."

"What. Are. You. Doing?" he repeated slowly, as if I were a child. His eyes were wide and stormy. He was absolutely furious.

"I —" My stomach sank with the realization that he'd probably heard at least part of my conversation with Nicholas — the one person on this earth I was not supposed to talk to. "Listen, I can ex —"

"No, I don't think you can," Hendricks said. Red blotches began to form on his neck and face. "Not this time."

Panic bubbled in my chest. "Jesse, if you would just —"

Hendricks stormed into the room, set the coffees on the desk, and picked up the surveillance photo. "Can you fucking read? The envelope is clearly marked for my eyes only. What makes you think you had the right to open it?"

"Why didn't you tell me you put Nicholas under surveillance?" I shot back.

"Because I didn't know if I could trust you not to tip him off. Turns out I made the right decision."

That was a dagger that pierced my very soul, mostly because he wasn't wrong. I'd really made a mess of things. "How much did you hear?"

"I heard enough." Hendricks grabbed the desk phone handset and began dialing. "I'm calling Captain Bailey."

I stood, picked my purse up off the desk, and tossed my RJPD access badge on the desk. "Don't bother. I'll just go."

I went. And I didn't look back.

CHAPTER 22

I stepped outside and decided not to go straight to my car. I was overwhelmed with a tsunami of thoughts and emotions I didn't completely understand, and I didn't trust myself to drive just yet. So I walked. The air was warm, sunglasses not optional. I followed Greenhaven Road three blocks east to where it ended at the Bourbon River, then used a footbridge to cross to the other side, and aimlessly followed a paved footpath that ran along the tree-lined riverbank.

The Bourbon River: along with the mighty Mississippi, with which it connected less than half a mile from where I stood, it was the lifeblood of River Junction. In the nineteenth century it drew enterprising businessmen from other parts of the region who wanted to harness the power of those rivers to make money. The Ainsleys, my family, settled here in the 1870s and built a wildly successful flour mill. The Fausts, Nicholas' family, arrived shortly thereafter and built a lumber enterprise to rival any in Minneapolis. There was plenty of room for both until a single bolt of lightning changed everything, shattering the bond between the two families and sparking a bitter feud. And the Bourbon River flowed through it all, a tenuous thread that bound the two families, for better or worse.

Powerful emotions coursed through my bloodstream as I walked: deep anger at Nicholas and profound sadness at the demise of our relationship; intense shame and gut-wrenching guilt over ruining Hendricks' chance at making detective; paralyzing fear for my mother's safety. All of which manifested in strange physical symptoms. My skin felt too tight on my body. My head felt like it might actually explode. My heart jittered inside my ribcage. I wanted to scream at the top of my lungs. If I had an ax, I probably could have chopped down a large tree without breaking a sweat. Mostly, though – mostly I just didn't know what to do about any of it. I'd never felt so helpless and afraid.

Colors changed in my peripheral vision; I glanced to my right and immediately recognized the stone-bound skeleton of the Ainsley Mansion partially hidden among wild brush and gnarled oak trees about a hundred feet back from the path. I stopped and stared for a moment, and realized I was looking at the rear portico door through which Edison and Morgan Faust had escaped just before I could pull the trigger of my father's gun and end Edison's reign of terror over my family. I looked ahead of me on the path; roughly quarter of a mile down I could just make out the Fortress' gray granite turret through the trees. They'd slipped out the back door and simply followed this path home. *Just as easy as pie*, I thought bitterly.

I turned to my left and looked out over the Bourbon River. It wasn't particularly wide at this point, maybe seventy-five feet across, but it looked deep and the murky water moved fast – fast enough to power entire industries in River Junction's heyday as a Victorian-era boomtown.

Movement on the other side of the river caught my eye. A small blue car drove along the riverbank through a large, mostly empty parcel of land. I watched it until it disappeared behind the crumbled ruins of an old building. *What's over there?* I wondered, then made a mental note to check it out when I was done here.

I stepped off the paved path and followed a narrow worn footpath through the brush, then walked through the back door of the Ainsley Mansion and into the room where Edison and Morgan had taken my dad after abducting him. I found myself standing in front of the fireplace, gazing at the MIA inscription once again. I pulled my glove off my right hand. *If I touch this and see Nicholas, I'll know. I'll know for sure.* I closed my eyes and laid my fingertips directly on the inscription.

At first I thought my touch short-circuited again because nothing had changed. I was still standing next to the fireplace and the MIA inscription. Even the way the sun cast shadows of the trees across the room was the same. A quick glance to my left, however, revealed one major difference: Nicholas. He was crisp and clear, which told me he'd been here very recently. *I bet he came here on Thursday after I asked him if he knew Mia.* He stood facing me, staring at the MIA inscription, and he wore all black: trousers, t-shirt, sneakers. His black hair was combed back from his pale, utterly expressionless face. He looked…sinister.

He looked like a Faust.

Then something strange happened. The silhouette I'd seen in a vision the day I rescued my dad faded in on top of Nicholas' face. The silhouette had been gray and fuzzy the first time I saw it; Hendricks and Chase had arrived before I could hone in and try to see whose face it was. Now, somehow, this second image grew brighter and clearer without any effort from me. The second face imposed itself over Nicholas' face, and I gasped.

They were the same face. It was Nicholas now, staring at the MIA inscription on the wall with his hands in his pockets, and Nicholas eleven years ago when he drew that inscription with a fat permanent marker.

At that moment I understood two things: first, despite what he'd said in his final texts to Mia, Nicholas loved her and baby Isabel. This inscription was his way of acknowledging that love without having to take real ownership of it. And second, he was absolutely capable of hurting them. If forced to own up to being Isabel's father, he would not have hesitated to dispatch them both to protect them and himself from his grandfather.

I was absolutely convinced that he had caused their disappearance. Why else would he come back here right after I asked him if he knew Mia?

I lifted my fingers from the old wooden slat, and Nicholas' faces evaporated. Tears came. I let them fall. My whole world had collapsed around me, and I didn't know what to do next.

I decided to go home to my family. That seemed like a good first step.

∞

Mimi was sliding a loaf of bread into the oven when I got there. The house smelled wonderful, but my stomach wanted none of it. I dragged myself into the kitchen and sat at the table, then laid my head on my folded arms.

"What's going on, love?" Her voice was sharp.

I debated telling her everything, then decided to spare her the details of how badly I'd fucked up the Mia Masterson case.

Instead I focused on my most immediate concern: my mother's safety. I raised my head and said, "Edison Faust knows where Mom is."

Mimi crossed the kitchen and sat next to me at the table. Her face was a patchwork quilt of emotions: surprise, concern, a touch of fear. "How?"

"Nicholas did some internet sleuthing and found the Uncle Carl connection. They have the address and everything."

"Oh, no," Mimi breathed.

"Kieran was right. Nicholas is helping his grandfather come after us. He used to protect us. I…I don't know what happened." A shaky sigh escaped me.

"My love, Edison Faust gets what he wants using threats, blackmail, extortion, and physical violence. Edison could be holding something over him, and he has no choice but to comply." She paused. "Or, perhaps Nicholas' basic nature just got the best of him."

The image of Nicholas standing emotionless in front of the MIA inscription materialized behind my eyes, and I shivered. I suspected the truth was somewhere in the middle – a combination of his family's unwavering hatred toward mine and his grandfather's words had finally poisoned Nicholas' beautiful soul.

"What do we do about Mom?"

Mimi patted my hand. "I'll take care of that. You don't worry about it anymore."

"Okay." Weariness washed over me; I didn't have the energy to argue or ask any more questions. All I wanted to do was lock myself in my childhood bedroom and sleep this whole nightmare away.

Mimi went back to her bread. I peeled myself from the kitchen table, poured myself a glass of wine, retrieved my phone from my purse, and made my way to the sun porch. It was warm and bright and quiet there; a little solitude was just what I needed.

Kieran was already there, reading a book and sipping a glass of iced tea. *So much for solitude,* I thought. I debated changing course and heading to the family room instead, but he looked up and saw me before I could.

"Hey," he said, peering at me over a pair of drugstore reading glasses. "Wow, you look terrible."

"Thanks for that," I said, too tired to come up with a witty comeback.

Kieran closed his book and patted the loveseat cushion next to him. "Come. Sit. Talk."

I collapsed next to him and took a healthy sip from my wineglass.

"What's going on?"

My mouth opened and words poured out before I could stop them. Unlike with Mimi, I didn't spare Kieran any of the details. My brother's face went through interesting changes as I described what I'd done to Hendricks and the smoking ruins of the Mia Masterson case, what I'd learned about Nicholas, and my fears for our mother's safety.

I finished talking and drained my wineglass. Curiously, I didn't feel compelled to pour another one. Kieran stared at his book cover, running his fingers over its raised lettering, lost in thought. Then he spoke.

"Wow."

"I know," I sighed. "I feel awful. I fucked everything up for Jesse."

Another pause. "Remember when Jesse brought you home the other day? Wednesday? You left him and me standing awkwardly in the driveway."

After we talked to Tom McCarthy, I thought. "Yeah."

"He thinks you hung the moon, Rae. He won't stay mad at you for very long."

My heart fluttered. "Did he say that?"

"He didn't have to. The sloppy look on his face as you walked inside told me everything I needed to know about the man."

I sighed. "That just makes me feel worse."

"You feel the same way about him, don't you?"

It was pointless to lie to my brother. Or to myself. "Yeah. Yeah, I do."

"Then what else do you need?"

I remembered Hendricks' words: *I didn't know if I could trust you not to tip him off. Turns out I made the right decision.* "He doesn't trust me, Kieran. And I can't say I blame him."

"Give him some time. And helping him solve the case wouldn't hurt either."

"I can't —"

Kieran interrupted me. "You can. You don't really need the backing of the River Junction PD to find Mia, Rae. You have the tools."

I realized my brother was right. There was nothing stopping me from investigating Mia's disappearance as a civilian. Armchair detectives with nothing but a computer and an internet connection did it all the time. And I had something none of them did: I had my touch.

I laid my head on Kieran's shoulder. "Thanks for the wisdom and guidance, bro."

"Of course. It's what wise older brothers do, don't ya know."

I smiled. "You do it well."

Kieran held up his book. "Annie sent this to me, insists I have something to read while I'm here. It's pretty good so far. And I'm waiting on a piping hot and buttered slice of Mimi's bread."

"I'll let you get back to it. I think I need a nap." I picked up my empty wineglass and headed for the kitchen.

"Have some bread," Kieran called after me. "It solves all of the world's problems!"

I chuckled and shook my head. I swung by the kitchen, set my glass in the sink, kissed Mimi's cheek, and headed to my room.

I slept for sixteen hours straight.

CHAPTER 23

My heart pounded as I guided my SUV into its assigned spot in my condo building's underground parking garage. I hadn't been to my own place in a week; a good night's sleep, a heavy dose of Mimi's strong coffee, and a suddenly empty schedule had given me the motivation I needed to come back and clean up the mess Morgan Faust had made. I rode the elevator up to the lobby and checked the mail, longing to be back in River Junction working the Mia Masterson case with Jesse Hendricks.

I wondered how Hendricks was doing, then pushed the thought from my mind. I appreciated Kieran's observations, but I didn't really believe Hendricks had feelings for me. I'd burned that bridge right to the ground. I sighed and used my key to open my mailbox.

As I flipped through the large pile of mail, something caught my eye outside the plate-glass window that overlooked the guest parking lot in front of the building. I glanced over, and my blood turned to ice when I recognized the large black SUV idling at the curb – and the man behind the wheel staring intently at me, his upper lip curled in a menacing sneer.

I should have been scared. That's why Morgan Faust was there after all, wasn't it? He'd followed me here to intimidate me, to strike fear into my heart. Instead a deadly calm poured over me like warm molasses, slowing my heartbeat and stilling my trembling hands. I turned and fully faced the window, giving Morgan my undivided attention.

The sneer disappeared from his scarred face, and his eyes widened. Then he shifted the SUV into drive and took off with a quick squeal of the tires. Satisfied, I closed and locked my mailbox, then headed back to the elevator for a ride up to my floor.

Everything so far, save for Morgan Faust's quick visit, felt totally normal. Ordinary. Which did not jibe with the turbulence in my gut. So much had happened – so much had *changed* – in the past two weeks that nothing felt right. I was an impostor in my own home. I longed to be back at my dad's house with my family. *That* was home – not this place.

I briefly considered knocking on Aaron and Kellie Long's door to let them know I was here and okay, but I could hear a puppy yapping and their two young daughters giggling through the door and decided not to disturb them. Instead I let myself into my own unit, and the state of it took my breath away. Again.

A week ago I'd come home from work after publishing my final story and resigning from my job to find my entire condo ransacked. Everything I owned had been overturned, strewn about, broken, and left in random piles while I was at the office. At the time I'd been too concerned with my father's safety to worry much about it, but now? Now, after a week of relative safety and comfort with my family at my dad's house, being here made me feel violated and fundamentally unsafe. And so very angry.

In the kitchen I came across a crumpled piece of paper lying on the floor. I picked it up, smoothed it out on the counter, and read the note scrawled in black marker: YOUR MOTHER OR YOUR FATHER. YOUR CHOICE. This note had been impaled to the wall with one of my kitchen knives, and it was the message Morgan Faust had really come here to deliver. When he found my condo empty, he ransacked the place just for fun.

None of this had to happen. Nicholas could have stopped it. The thought unleashed pure, white-hot rage into my bloodstream, kick-starting my heart into a manic pace. The man who had professed to love me had been working against me. He'd betrayed me. Why? I remembered what Mimi had said: *Edison Faust gets what he wants using threats, blackmail, extortion, and physical violence. Edison could be holding something over him, and he has no choice but to comply.* But that excuse rang hollow to me. Nicholas' love for me should have trumped everything. He'd promised me it would. And his involvement with Mia Masterson still troubled me.

I wasn't done with Nicholas yet. I retrieved my phone from my purse and composed a text message to Nicholas with burning fingertips: We need to talk. Meet me at Ainsley Mansion. Noon. Then, on a whim, I shot a quick message to Hendricks: I'm sorry, Jesse. For everything. I'm meeting N at Ainsley Mansion at noon to get some answers, hoping to help you salvage your case.

I glanced at the time: 10:30. It was time to go.

∞

I parked my SUV almost exactly where Hendricks and Chase had parked their cruiser after being summoned when a neighbor heard my gunshot. *My god, was that really a week ago?* It felt like yesterday and forever ago.

I didn't see Nicholas' red Audi, but that didn't mean anything; his grandfather's house was just a quarter of a mile away. Easy walking distance. As I approached the house, I ticked off in my head all the questions I would ask Nicholas:

Why are you helping your grandfather track down my mother?

Do you still love me?

Why did you lie to me about Mia?

Are you Isabel's father?

Did you kill them?

Where are they?

I dreaded the answers. I really did. But I needed to know.

I stepped through the opening that had once been the grand front door and stopped for a moment. Listened. Hearing nothing, I slowly followed the main hallway toward the back of the structure, poking my head into empty rooms as I went. Sweat dripped down my back. "Nicholas?"

Silence. I shivered despite the oppressive summer heat and humidity. *Rain coming soon,* I thought randomly.

I entered the back room, and there he was. He looked exactly like he had in my vision: black pants, t-shirt and shoes, his normally wild black hair slicked back from his forehead. He stood near the fireplace – and the back door – watching me impassively.

My stomach dropped, and I stopped just inside the door. The room suddenly seemed enormous, a gulf between us. "Hey."

Nicholas lifted his chin a bit, but his expression didn't change.

"I – ah, I was hoping we could talk." I tried to control the tremble in my voice.

"You were pretty fucking clear on the phone yesterday." I could have sworn his voice sounded deeper, and it was smooth

212

as silk. No sign of nervousness. "What more could you possibly have to say?"

I took a couple steps toward him. My heart galloped in my chest. "I just want to know why."

The beginnings of a frown wrinkled his forehead. "Why what?"

I moved another step or two further into the room. "Why you turned against me. From the beginning you promised me you'd do everything you could to protect me and my family from your grandfather. You *promised*. You didn't stop him from kidnapping my dad, and you're helping him find my mom. What the actual fuck?" I realized I was shouting. I didn't care.

Nicholas just stood there, hands in the pockets of his black trousers, and stared at me.

"When did you decide you don't love me anymore?" I asked.

He blinked and lowered his head for a moment, then raised it again. "I never stopped loving you, Rae. I just –" He didn't finish his sentence.

"You just what?"

Nicholas sighed. "Edison is cutting me in on Jack Hughes' gold. I help him find it, I get a third of the take. That's the deal."

My heart shattered in my chest. "What?" I half-whispered.

He crossed the room with the speed and stealth of a black cat, and took my gloved hands in his. "I'm doing it for *us*, baby. We'll take the money and live like royalty, just you and me, away from this shithole town and our shithole families. We'll be free, Rae. Just like we've always talked about." He pulled me into an awkward hug. "We'll be *free*."

Two weeks ago this would have been music to my ears; I'd been waiting eleven years to hear it. Now it just sounded like a steaming pile of fresh cowshit. Thunderstruck, I pushed him away. "You're risking my mom's life over gold that nobody's sure actually exists? Are – are you *kidding* me?"

I might as well have told him the earth was flat. "It exists, Rae. You just wait. Danielle will tell us where it is, and we'll be millionaires."

"And what does my mother get for her trouble?" I was shouting again, and this time I was seeing red. "Do you honestly think some imaginary *gold* is going to convince me to stand by and let Edison make her his...his *servant*? So he can force her to use her touch for his own benefit?" I was so upset I could hardly breathe; my throat made a scary squealing sound with every heaving inhale. "Fuck you if that's what you think. You don't fucking know me at all."

Nicholas' face darkened. At that moment he looked frighteningly like his grandfather. So much so that I suddenly found myself without words. A rare occurrence.

We stood and stared at each other, each of us daring the other to make the next move.

I should have turned and walked away then. Instead I decided, rather foolishly, that I didn't yet have all the answers I came here for. "Why did you lie to me about Mia?"

Nicholas rolled his eyes like a teenage girl. "Jesus, Raegan, stop badgering me about Mia. I told you, I had nothing to do with that."

"You threatened to kill her the night before she went missing," I pointed out.

"She pissed me off. That doesn't mean I did anything to her."

My breath caught in my throat; this was the first time he'd acknowledged having any interaction with Mia since about the year 2000. "Gee, Nicholas, I thought you hadn't seen or talked to her since high school." I was being sarcastic and petty. I couldn't help myself.

His eyes and his nostrils flared. "You want to watch your mouth, Raegan. You know nothing."

"I know more than you think," I shot back. I could have turned and left at this point, but I was so wound up that I wanted to get some kind of a reaction out of Nicholas. I was trying to pick a fight. "You loved her. That's why you drew that." I pointed at the MIA inscription. "So why did you kill Mia and baby Isabel and just go on with your life as if neither had ever existed?"

Nicholas' face went a dark shade of red that flirted with burgundy. His aloof demeanor was entirely gone. I'd never seen him so angry.

"You and I met a month later. And never in all our time together did you ever once mention Mia Masterson's name." I paused, breathing heavily, then went straight to the heart of it all. "Where did you hide their bodies, Nicholas?"

Nicholas' eyebrows came together and his top lip curled. He looked exactly like his father, but without the scar. Then his left arm shot out like a piston and he plunged his hand deep into my hair. I was so shocked that I couldn't resist when he pulled my body firmly against his, immobilizing me, and grabbed my throat with his right hand. He simultaneously squeezed, digging his fingers into my neck, and pushed, pinching my windpipe closed. My mouth opened and my eyes bulged with my fruitless efforts to breathe. I clutched at his hand, trying to pry his fingers away from my throat. Pressure built in my head and my lungs burned.

Nicholas brought my face so close to his that I could feel his carrion breath against my skin. "I didn't kill that bitch, but I should have," he snarled. This wasn't the Nicholas I'd loved. That Nicholas, the one who'd been raised by his mother to be kind and caring and everything a Faust wasn't, was gone. This Nicholas, whose eyes swirled with deep, dark evil, was a Faust to the core. This was the Nicholas behind the awful last texts Mia Masterson had received before she disappeared.

I tried to say his name, but I couldn't produce a single noise. So I slowly mouthed it, hoping he would see. Hoping for mercy. *Nicholas. Nicholas. Nicholas.* My vision was turning gray at the edges. My lungs burst into flame. My arms and hands lost strength and fell to my sides. My head was seconds away from popping like a Fourth of July cherry bomb.

This is it. I'm going to die. I'm dying.

The gray drifted across my sight like a dense fog, obliterating everything.

I waited for death to arrive and take away the pain.

CHAPTER 24

I was pretty sure I was dead.

"Raegan."

My throat and my chest hurt. My head throbbed. Huh. I didn't know dead people could feel pain.

"Stay with me, Raegan."

I realized I was gasping for air. Coughing. Breathing. But how? Wasn't I dead?

"Come on, Raegan. Wake up."

My eyelids popped open like window shades. I was lying on the floor of the Ainsley Mansion. Panic set in. Where was Nicholas? Oh god. I wasn't dead. He'd failed to kill me. Would he come back and finish the job? I frantically tried to sit up, but didn't have the strength and had to lie back down. I wildly turned my head left and right, trying to see everything, trying to prepare for another attack.

"Hey. Hey, calm down. I'm here."

That voice. I knew that voice. But where was it coming from? "J–Jesse?" I croaked through pins and needles in my throat. *Damn, that hurts.*

Hendricks' face, his beautiful face, moved into my field of vision from behind me. I realized my head was cradled in his lap. "Hey," he said, and gave me an upside-down smile.

I tried again to scramble to a sitting position, successful this time. Hendricks caught me before my muscles could fail, and wrapped me tight in his warm, strong arms. "I got you."

Sweet relief and paralyzing fear overwhelmed me, and I dissolved into hysterics. I'd walked in here and let Nicholas almost take me away from my family. I started to imagine a scene exactly like the vision I'd had of Hendricks and his mom learning about the death of his girlfriend. Only now it was my family receiving the news that I'd died. Mimi might collapse. Kieran might punch a hole in the wall. My dad...

I pushed the image away. It was too upsetting.

How could I have been so stupid?

Hendricks held me and stroked my hair as I wailed. My voice sounded broken and the pain in my throat was unlike anything I'd ever experienced. "It's okay, you're okay, I've got you," he soothed.

After several minutes I was all cried out, left with gritty red eyes, a snotty nose, and a tear-streaked face. Hendricks gently cradled my face in his hands and looked me in the eyes. "Better?"

I nodded, wiped my face, and sniffled. Even that hurt.

"Okay. Good." His voice shook. He dropped his eyes to my neck. "You're going to have some gnarly bruises there." He helped me move a few feet to the nearest wall, and we sat shoulder-to-shoulder against it.

"God, you gave me a scare," he said.

"I'm sorry," I rasped.

"You don't need me to tell you that you made a mistake here, do you?"

I shook my head, and tears threatened again. "No. I feel so stupid."

"Thank god you texted me," Hendricks said. "I was meeting with Captain Bailey when I got your text, and I came as soon as she was done with me. I was just in time to see Nicholas Faust run out that back door when he heard me coming."

"You had to meet with Bailey on a Sunday?"

"Yeah. It isn't often that she will interrupt a summer weekend to come into the office. I'm special that way, I guess."

Oh, no. "What did she say?"

Hendricks lifted a shoulder, then dropped it. "She's shutting down the Mia Masterson investigation. Moving me back to patrol." He sighed. "So much for making detective."

My eyes burned. "You have no idea how sorry I am, Jesse. I completely ruined everything for you."

Hendricks reached over and took my hand, intertwining my fingers with his. His touch felt nice, even through my gloves. We sat in silence for a few minutes, both lost in our own thoughts.

I stared across the room at the back door through which Nicholas had made his escape, and remembered my walk along the river the day before. "Hey, I have a question."

Hendricks gently squeezed my fingers as he came back from whatever mental train he'd been on. "What's that?"

I pointed. "If you go out that door and through some trees, you end up on a path that goes along the river. On the other side of the river is a big parcel of land that looks like it's abandoned. Do you know what it is?"

He nodded. "Yeah, that's the old Faust Lumber site. The company went out of business in the 1940s, but the family still owns the land. Edison just lets the place sit there and rot." He looked up and gestured around the room we were in. "Like your family does with this place. Kids like to hang out over there and explore – you should see all the graffiti – and locals on the south side of town have taken to driving through as a shortcut to downtown rather than dealing with the stoplights on Fourth Avenue. Everyone calls it Bourbon Street, like in New Orleans."

That explained the blue car I'd seen yesterday. "Huh." I tried to move on, but something in my brain wouldn't let it go. *South side of town.* Why was that important? I called up a mental image of the River Junction wall map we'd hung in our war room…and that's when it hit me. I yanked my hand out of Hendricks' and sat up straight.

"What is it?" he asked, startled.

"I talked to Lyle Allister yesterday morning before you got to the station. Did you see the notes I left on the desk?" It hurt like hell to talk, and I sounded like a two-pack-a-day smoker.

"I saw them," he admitted. "But I couldn't read them. You should have been a doctor with that scribble."

I waved this away. "Lyle said that Mia was at River Drug right when it opened on the day she went missing. She needed formula for baby Isabel. That's where she was going when James Locke saw her leave her house. Would she have taken Bourbon Street to get there?"

Understanding dawned on Hendricks' face, and he looked at me with wide eyes. "Goddamn straight she would have."

"She left River Drug at eight-fifteen and made her last call to the Junction Medical Clinic at eight-seventeen. Both Lyle and James mentioned that she looked ill. Would she have taken Bourbon Street to get to the clinic from the drugstore?"

Hendricks nodded, eyes even wider.

I slowly and painstakingly stood up. My whole body hurt. "Let's go."

Hendricks popped up with no effort at all. "I'll drive."

∞

Faust Lumber had once stood on roughly five acres of prime riverfront property. During its heyday in the early twentieth century, Stefan Faust ran a busy sawmill, turning pine logs that his lumberjacks cut and sent down the Bourbon River into boards and planks suitable for building houses and other structures. By the end of Faust Lumber's tenure, Minnesota forests were tapped out and lumber barons had moved their milling operations west. Stefan converted his operations to a wholesale lumberyard in early 1938, helping Faust Lumber survive the last part of the Great Depression. When the United States was drawn into World War II in 1941, available resources were directed to supporting the war effort. The final blow was the death of Stefan Faust at the hands of his wife in 1942. Stefan's son Benedict inherited the company and finally closed its doors in 1943.

Benedict Faust, who never married after he was rejected by my great-grandmother Grace Ainsley, retreated to the Fortress with his out-of-wedlock son Edison. He killed himself in 1960, a month after Grace's sudden and unexplained passing. Edison Faust couldn't be bothered with maintaining the Faust Lumber property, and it was left to deteriorate – much to the chagrin of city officials, who had been petitioning Edison to sell them the land for years. They intended to turn it into a large riverside park.

I peered through the passenger-side window of Hendricks' pickup at the wreckage that had once been a thriving business. Not much remained of the structures. A brick building close to the river, which I imagined once housed the office, lay in crumbling ruins. A large collapsed pile of broken and weathered boards, along with crumpled sheets of rusty corrugated steel, sat about a hundred feet away. Clumps of tall weeds grew from the pile, and the whole thing was encircled by an old chain-link fence and signs that said STAY OUT and NO TRESPASSING. Naturally the fence had been cut and bent open in a couple of places, allowing people to go in and explore. *The shed where they stored some of the lumber?* I wondered.

Behind that, a huge yard full of piles of ancient ruined lumber lay within the perimeter of what I thought might once have been a tall wooden fence. All that remained of the fence were concrete pilings. The rotted wood piles were covered in weeds and painted thick with beautiful spray paint graffiti. The artwork reminded me of a story I'd done for the Daily News & Review a few years back about urban art and its place in our cities. It had been a rare venture outside the world of crime, and Lou Brown had loved the results. "Maybe I should move you to the Arts desk," he'd growled. I laughed and politely declined. The art world wasn't really for me, but I'd been a fan of urban art ever since I'd had the opportunity to meet and interview some of the artists behind the masterpieces.

Bourbon Street was nothing more than a gravel path carved by cars that had created their own road through the site. It branched off from dead-end Lyon Street to the south and wound about half a mile north along the river before reconnecting with First Avenue, which led directly downtown. Cars were forced to navigate between the ruined office building and the collapsed shed, bringing them precariously close to the river's edge before jogging back behind the yard and onto dry land.

Hendricks parked on a patch of scrubby grass on the Lyon Street end and we both got out of the vehicle. With him on the far side and me closer to the river, we began to walk the entire length of Bourbon Street. I wasn't very hopeful; nearly eleven years had passed since Mia may have driven through here. The chances of finding any evidence were basically zero.

But we had to try. For her sake, and for ours.

From the dead end barrier on Lyon Street to the ruins of the office building, Hendricks and I walked slowly, eyes on the ground. The sun beat down on us, turning our necks and scalps red, but still we walked on. There were more cigarette butts, beer bottles and empty shot liquor bottles than we could count – but every once in a while something different would catch our eyes and we'd stop to examine it.

"Broken sunglasses," Hendricks called out, holding up a pair of shattered aviators.

I pulled a torn and faded pair of ladies' panties out from under a piece of scrap wood. "Gross," I said. Hendricks chuckled.

It went on like that for twenty minutes or so, until we reached the rough midpoint of Bourbon Street, on the north end of the ruined office building. I stopped, hot and sweaty, still in quite a bit of pain, and tied my hair up in a messy bun. I sighed and put my hands on my hips, feeling hopeless.

Something flashed in my peripheral vision. It was a very small flash, but it was bright enough to catch my attention and pique my curiosity. It had come from somewhere near or under the crumbled brick of what remained of the office building's north wall. I went to the area and knelt, examining the ground for something that might reflect the sunlight. I brushed aside a bit of gravel, and there, in a slight depression in the ground and sheltered by the brick, lay a delicate necklace.

"Jesse!" I called. "I found something!"

Hendricks, who had been poking around in the ruins of the old storage shed, jogged over to me. "What is it?"

I carefully tweezed the tarnished chain between my right pointer finger and thumb and lifted the necklace from the ground. The fiery sun pendant, its center inexplicably shinier than the rest of the necklace, flashed as it twisted in the slight breeze.

"Holy shit," Hendricks breathed. "Do you think –"

"It's Mia's. She was wearing this necklace in the vision I had when I touched her horse figurine."

"Holy shit," he said again.

I used my teeth to pull the glove off my left hand, then looked at Hendricks. "Here goes nothing."

He watched, wide-eyed, as I placed the necklace in my bare hand and closed my eyes.

CHAPTER 25

Bourbon Street stretched in front of me through the windshield as Mia drove her Jeep around the barrier at the end of First Avenue, heading south. The crumbled remains of the office building lay ahead.

The view shifted when Mia turned toward the backseat. Baby Isabel lay in her carseat/carrier on the passenger side, red-faced and squirming, clearly uncomfortable. She wore tiny striped sleeper pajamas with a yellow duck embroidered on them and had a head full of fine jet-black hair. There was no question who her father was. My heart broke a little.

I didn't have children of my own so I wasn't sure, but I thought Isabel should have been facing the rear of the car instead of the front. I also noticed that the upper clip of the seat's harness wasn't fastened at the baby's chest. All of the windows I could see were rolled down halfway, probably to take advantage of the crisp late-September air.

Mia returned her attention to the road in front of her and continued down Bourbon Street. Just as the Jeep reached the office building, it suddenly stopped. Mia got out of the car, stumbled to the crumbled brick wall, braced herself against it, and vomited. Partially digested oatmeal followed by thick yellow bile splattered on the dirt and weeds next to the brick. Mia's violent retching somehow loosened her necklace, and it slipped from her neck. The sensation of falling made my stomach turn.

From my new vantage point on the ground where I would find the necklace eleven years later, I watched Mia get back into her Jeep and continue south down Bourbon Street, around the other side of the office building, and disappear from view.

∞

I opened my eyes, transferred the necklace to my other hand, and put my glove back on.

"What did you see?" Hendricks asked.

"Mia was sick," I confirmed. "She lost her necklace when she stopped right here to throw up."

"She had baby Isabel with her, right?"

I nodded. "The baby looked like she wasn't feeling well either." I didn't offer up my opinion that Nicholas was almost certainly Isabel's father. "She was so...so *tiny*."

Hendricks held out a small clear plastic baggie. "I remembered to grab a few of these before I got out of the truck," he said. I dropped the necklace into it, and he sealed it and stashed it in the pocket of his khaki shorts.

We had been working our search of Bourbon Street from south to north. I decided to follow the path Mia's car had taken after she stopped to throw up and turned around to head south again. Hendricks continued north to make sure we didn't miss anything from the beginning of Mia's journey.

A little ways past the south side of the office building, I saw something I hadn't noticed on my way by the first time: a big old pothole. It looked like it'd been there a long time, growing unchecked as passing cars chipped away at its edges, rain and snow eroded the dirt and gravel, and nobody bothered to fix it. It sat just a few yards away from the section of Bourbon Street that ran closest to the river. *I wonder…*

I stopped next to the pothole and looked around, reasoning that if this hole was here in 2010 and Mia ran over it on her way through, maybe something fell off her Jeep. It was possible; the Faust Lumber site was completely neglected and potholes were known to cause thousands of dollars' worth of damage to vehicles. I spied a nearby pile of wrecked pallets and went to check it out. There, almost completely concealed by weeds, lay a weather-worn sideview mirror from a vehicle. I couldn't believe my luck.

I carefully picked it up and examined it. It appeared to have broken off from the base at the swivel that allowed the mirror to fold in to prevent damage in parking lots and car washes. The mirror was cracked and filthy and the cover was black, the same color as Mia's Jeep Liberty. Could this be from her car?

There was only one way to find out.

Once again I used my teeth to remove a glove, and I laid my bare fingertips on the mirror's surface to see what might have happened to Mia and Isabel next.

∞

The Jeep rounded the south end of the office building and proceeded toward the ruined shed — and the riverbank — at a faster clip than before. I could see Mia's face now, and she did not look well at all. Her hair was greasy and plastered to her scalp. She was deathly pale, her eyes were sunken, and she appeared to have trouble keeping her eyes open. I couldn't see the baby.

Suddenly Mia sat up stick-straight. Her grip on the steering wheel tightened until her knuckles were white, and her eyes rolled back in her head. Her entire body jerked violently. She relaxed for a second or two, and then her body seized again, causing her to push the accelerator to the floor and yank the wheel hard to the left. Her vehicle hit the pothole going at least thirty miles an hour; I had the sensation of falling again as the mirror separated from the driver's side door, landed on the ground, and bounced, coming to rest against the pile of pallets.

I watched in horror as Mia's Jeep, still accelerating, drove directly into the Bourbon River. It made an incredible splash and the vehicle sank quickly, aided by the open windows. Within a minute the Jeep was gone, sunk to the river's depths.

I never saw Mia try to escape.

∞

"No!" I cried, my voice hoarse, letting the mirror fall from my fingers and clatter to the gravel.

"Raegan?" Jesse's voice bounced as he ran to me. "What's wrong?" He knelt next to me and laid a hand on my sweaty back.

I pointed. "They're in the river."

Hendricks' eyes grew to roughly the size of Cadillac hubcaps as he looked from my face to the river to the side mirror at my feet and back to my face. "They're – what?"

"Mia had a seizure right here and drove her car into the Bourbon River," I rasped. "She never got out. Neither did the baby."

Hendricks, eyes still wide, rubbed his face. "Holy shit," he muttered. He looked again at the mirror. "Did you find that?"

I nodded. "It's from Mia's car. It fell off when she ran over that pothole."

Hendricks stood, fished his cellphone from the other pocket of his shorts, and made a call. "Captain Bailey, it's Jesse Hendricks. I'm sorry to bug you again on a Sunday, but I'm out at the Faust Lumber site with Raegan and…we think we know where Mia Masterson is."

I stood too and listened as Hendricks explained the entire incredible story to Bailey – who, to her credit, let him speak without interruption.

When he finished, she spoke. Hendricks glanced at me. "Yes ma'am, she used her ability to see what happened, but the evidence she found is more than enough to get a team out here. Okay. Okay. We'll wait for them. Thank you, Captain." He rang off. Then he stood and extended a hand. "Come on, let's go wait in the truck."

We walked back to his truck in silence, hand in hand. He started it up and cranked the air conditioning, then moved closer to the collapsed shed and parked where it would be out of the way but still offered a view of the river where Mia's car had gone in. Then he turned and gazed at me with fiery eyes. "You are incredible, did you know that?"

I responded with a small smile. "Yeah, I know." I croaked. My throat still hurt, but the trauma of what had happened with Nicholas paled in comparison to the excitement of finally knowing what had happened to Mia and Isabel Masterson,

We were going to bring them home.

Hendricks reached across the console and gently stroked my face. His touch left fiery trails on my cheeks. "I'd like to kiss you," he murmured.

"Okay," I whispered.

He leaned in and pressed his lips against mine. I closed my eyes and savored his warmth. He very gently ran his fingers over the bruises on my neck while he explored my lips with his, and my hand gripped his upper arm, trying to pull him closer.

This felt different than before. This wasn't drunken pawing. This was real.

The crunch of rolling tires on the gravel of Bourbon Street finally separated us. Officers Cory Chase and Ricardo Lopez pulled up in their marked RJPD cruiser. "Here we go," Hendricks muttered. "You stay here, okay?"

I nodded; Chase and Lopez didn't know about my touch, and given the fact that I was still in trouble with Captain Bailey, it made sense that I stay out of conversations with the officers.

Hendricks hopped out of his truck and approached his partner and Lopez. I stayed in the air conditioning and watched as he told them what had happened to Mia. I knew he was spinning the story as an educated guess based on the evidence we'd found. He pulled the baggie containing Mia's necklace from his pocket and handed it to Chase, who looked rather baffled, and sent Lopez to collect the side mirror lying on the ground near the pallets. At that moment an unmarked car driven by Detective Sergeant Carter Rooney, a Greenhaven County Sheriff's Department tactical van containing divers and equipment, a van marked MEDICAL EXAMINER, and a big tow truck pulled in. Rooney assumed command of the scene, and Hendricks made his way back to me. He gestured for me to come out of the pickup truck, so I did. He wrapped an arm around my shoulders as we watched two divers suit up, make their way to the water, and submerge themselves.

It didn't take long. Within five minutes one of the divers surfaced about fifteen feet from shore, removed the oxygen regulator from his mouth, and shouted "We've got it!" A ripple of excitement went through everyone, and the tow truck driver readied his steel cable and winch. The cable was hooked to the Jeep's rear axle and the winch whined. Everyone watched somberly, hats removed, as Mia Masterson's black Jeep Liberty, covered in mud and river slime and missing its driver side mirror but otherwise completely intact, slowly emerged from the depths of the Bourbon River. My heart pounded in my chest, and tears ran down Hendricks' face.

Once the vehicle was fully on land, Rooney stepped up to the driver's side window and shone his flashlight inside. "We've got bones," he announced through his bushy mustache. "Hendricks! What did you say Mia was wearing when she went missing?"

"Black yoga pants and a white cropped shirt, boss," Hendricks called back.

Rooney leaned into the cab of the ruined SUV. "Yep, I've got what looks like black spandex here."

"That shit does not decompose," Hendricks said in a low voice.

"Autopsy will confirm, but I'm pretty confident in saying we just found Mia Masterson." Then he inspected the backseat. "I see an infant carseat, but —" he paused. "But no infant bones."

"We didn't see any bones on the riverbottom," one of the divers said as he toweled off.

Thunderstruck silence descended upon the scene. Hendricks left my side and stormed over to the Jeep. "What do you mean?" he shouted. "The baby's not in there?"

Rooney stepped aside and let Hendricks look inside the car. Hendricks took Rooney's flashlight and shone it all throughout the Jeep's cab and cargo area. His shoulders slumped and he handed the flashlight back to Rooney. Then he turned to look at me.

"The baby is gone."

∞

An hour later, Mia's remains had been carefully removed, placed in a medical examiner's bodybag, and taken to the morgue. Her Jeep had been put on the tow truck's flatbed and hauled out to the RJPD's garage for further examination. All of the police vehicles were gone. Hendricks and I lingered at the Faust Lumber site, sitting on the open tailgate of his pickup.

"Where could a four-day-old infant go?" Hendricks wondered out loud. He'd removed the glove from my right hand and held it in both of his. Our skin-to-skin touch greatly amplified all of my emotions because he was experiencing them too. One second I thought I might cry, the next second I wanted to laugh. We were riding the rollercoaster vibes of finding Mia and not finding baby Isabel.

I leaned my head against his shoulder and sighed, enjoying his warmth and his company. "I don't know," I said. And then I remembered something I saw in my sideview mirror vision. "Mia didn't have baby Isabel buckled into her carseat properly."

"Yeah, the clip on the harness straps was undone," he said. "I saw that. She must be in the water somewhere."

It hurt my heart to imagine it, so I chose to be optimistic. "The diver said they didn't see any bones near the car."

Hendricks pushed air through his lips. "Come on, let's go."

We headed back to his place. It was coming up on dinnertime, but neither of us was hungry. Instead we sat on the couch where I'd slept off a hard-drinking night earlier in the week and talked.

It wasn't long before talking turned to fooling around, and soon after that we moved to his bed and made love.

Afterward, wrapped protectively in Jesse Hendricks' arms, I slept deeply and soundly for the first time in weeks.

I was where I was meant to be.

Monday, July 19, 2021

CHAPTER 26

Oh, look, a lovely little duck pond.

Scratch that, it's a lovely little rubber duckie pond.

The water's surface is covered with bright yellow rubber duckies. Big ones, little ones, all the rubber duckies are here.

I want to swim with them.

They're all looking at me and smiling. They're so cute!

The water's warm.

They're all swimming around me in a big circle. Round and round they go. Maybe I –

Ouch! That one just bit me!

Ouch! That one made me bleed.

I didn't know their bills could be so sharp.

Ouch!

Ouch!

Ow –

∞

I jerked awake. Hendricks snorted and turned over on his side. *What the hell?*

I stared at the ceiling and waited for my heart to slow down. Bright morning light shone around the edges of Hendricks' light-blocking curtains.

The rubber duckie dream confounded me. I couldn't figure out why I would have such a bizarre dream about something so…ordinary. What was my subconscious trying to tell me?

I had no idea.

I turned onto my side and spooned Hendricks, snaking my arm around his chest and soaking in his warmth. He smelled like sun-soaked beach sand. I relaxed and let my mind wander, hoping to fall back into blessed sleep.

Where is baby Isabel?

She was in the car when it went into the river.

Baby in the river. Where have I read about that before?

Oh, right. Todd sent me all those articles about Angel Baby.

They found Angel Baby in the Mississippi River, though.

Isabel went into the Bourbon River.

Wait. The Bourbon River connects with the Mississippi not far from the Ainsley Mansion.

Yellow. Yellow ducks.

Do you think…?

I abruptly sat up, accidentally waking Hendricks in the process. "Wha–? What are you doing?" he asked sleepily.

I rolled out of bed and went looking for my phone. "I have to call Lyle Allister." I knew what I'd seen in my vision, but needed the pharmacist to verify that he'd seen the same thing. I finally found my purse on the bedroom floor, grabbed my phone, and sat on the edge of the bed.

"Why?"

I shook my head as I dialed the River Drug phone number. It rang once before Allister himself answered. "Hello, Ms.

O'Rourke," he greeted me after I identified myself. "What can I help you with today?"

"Mr. Allister, do you remember what Mia Masterson's baby was wearing when they came into your store before they went missing?"

Allister thought for a moment. "Yes, she was wearing a sleeper with yellow stripes on it. It had a little yellow duck embroidered on the chest. I remember Lucy fawning over how cute it was. I don't know about such things, myself."

I released breath I hadn't realized I was holding. "Thank you, Mr. Allister. I appreciate your help." I rang off and stared at the bedspread without seeing it.

"Raegan?" Hendricks was sitting up now, watching me with some concern.

Isabel Masterson had been wearing sleeper pajamas with a little yellow duck on them when she went into the Bourbon River on September 22, 2010.

Lorenzo Garcia found the body of Angel Baby while fishing in the Mississippi River three days later. The pajamas had a little yellow duck on them, he'd said.

I turned and looked at Hendricks. "Isabel Masterson is Angel Baby," I said.

"What does that mean, exactly?"

I told him the story of Minneapolis' famous Angel Baby. By the time I was done, his eyes were back to Cadillac hubcap size. "Holy shit."

"We already know that Isabel wasn't properly buckled into her carseat. Mia also had all the windows in her car open. Isabel was brand-new and so tiny. I think after the car sank, the river current pulled her body out of her carseat, through the open window, and sent her downstream."

Hendricks looked a little sick. "There's a dam on the Mississippi between here and Minneapolis. Isabel would have –" he couldn't finish.

I nodded. "The newspaper articles mentioned that her body was pretty scraped up and her pajamas torn. That would explain it."

"So what do we do?"

I took his hands. "What *you're* going to do is get up, get dressed, and take all of this information to Captain Bailey. You just solved two huge high-profile cases. There's no way she won't make you a detective now."

Hendricks shook his head. "I can't do that, Raegan. You solved these cases, not me."

"You can, and you will." I grasped his face and kissed him. "Because I have to go home."

CHAPTER 27

After Hendricks dropped me off at my car, I headed back to my dad's house. Since my nearly fatal run-in with Nicholas yesterday, I wanted to make sure everything there was all right.

I thought about Nicholas on the drive home. He'd had me so thoroughly bamboozled for a long time, believing he and I could have had a future together. I should have known better — *would* have known better if my stupid naive heart hadn't been in the way. Ainsley women and Faust men could never truly live in harmony.

Maybe someday I would be able to forgive myself for being such a damn fool. I gently touched my bruised and inflamed neck and winced; today would not be that day.

I wasn't looking forward to having to explain those bruises to my family — Mimi especially, because she'd been right all along. *They're all unpredictable and dangerous. Especially when they're angry.*

I sighed and pushed all thoughts of Nicholas away. I wanted to focus on something that had real potential: Jesse Hendricks. Remembering our night of passion brought a smile back to my face.

I hope things are going well with Bailey, I thought. I knew Hendricks wouldn't go in there and try to convince her that he'd solved the

Mia Masterson and Angel Baby cases on his own. She already knew that I'd been at the Faust Lumber site with him yesterday and found the evidence that led us to Mia's submerged Jeep. I just hoped that she would understand that I couldn't have done any of it without him.

She wasn't stupid; I thought she did.

Just then, as if he knew I was thinking about him, Hendricks called. I answered hands-free. "Hey you."

"Hey yourself." His deep, soothing voice surrounded me like a fluffy cloud. "I thought you'd like to know what Mia's preliminary autopsy report says."

"You better believe I do. I want to know what she was so sick with."

"The primary cause of death is freshwater drowning, but the M.E. is pretty sure he knows what's behind the seizures that caused her to drive into the Bourbon River."

"And that is?"

I heard paper shuffling. "A rare pregnancy complication called HELLP syndrome." He pronounced this "help" and then spelled it out for me. "It's related to preeclampsia and it seriously messes with blood and liver function. Nobody knows what causes it. Symptoms include abdominal pain, swelling, seizures."

"Mia had all that," I said.

"Yes, and the sad thing is, it's treatable. Even after childbirth."

"If she'd only made it to the clinic. Oh god, poor Mia."

"Yes. The autopsy report is not final, but given her symptoms and the fact that she'd just given birth, he's like ninety-five percent sure."

It was an accident, I thought. *Betrayed by her own body because she had a baby.* I couldn't wrap my head around it. It was so sad.

Hendricks changed the subject. "I'm meeting with Bailey in an hour. Are you sure you don't want to be here for this?"

"You got this," I said. "I'm almost to my dad's house. Call me after your meeting and let me know how it went."

Hendricks promised he would, and the call ended. I rounded the curve and saw my dad's SUV sitting in the driveway. *He's home!* He'd been gone for a few days, and Mimi wouldn't tell Kieran and me where he was.

I parked next to his car and went inside. The kitchen was empty, but I heard voices and followed them to the back porch. I got as far as the door and stopped, confused. Mimi, Kieran, and my dad stood in a tight huddle in the middle of the warm, sun-drenched room.

"What's going on?" I asked.

They all looked at me with shining eyes. Then my dad stepped to the side, revealing a slender figure with curly shoulder-length platinum hair. She turned around to face me and smiled.

"M–Mom?" I stammered.

"Hi baby," she said. She looked exactly as she had on the video call, but in real life she was more petite than I expected, her wrinkles were more pronounced, her lips were a little thinner, her eyes were a bit sunken with age.

My god, she was beautiful.

I stepped tentatively into the room, still not completely sure I believed what I was seeing. I looked at Mimi, who nodded, and my dad, who held out his hand.

"Are–are you really here?" I asked.

"She really is," Kieran said. He had an arm around her slim shoulders, and his face was joyful.

Danielle stepped forward and raised her arms, inviting me in for a hug. It was an invitation I gladly accepted. I crossed the room and walked into her arms, wrapping my own around her and holding her tight. The tears were flowing before I even knew they were there. "I can't believe you're here," I sobbed.

"I'm so happy to be here, baby," she crooned as she stroked my hair.

It took me a few minutes to calm down. When I finally did, Danielle released me and we all sat. Mom and Dad were on the loveseat holding hands (an adorable sight I thought I might never get over), and Mimi took a cushioned cane chair. Kieran and I pulled up folding chairs. It was an honest-to-god family meeting, with the whole family for the first time.

I didn't wait around for small talk. "Is this where you've been the last few days, Dad?"

"Your mother and I decided after Thursday's video call that it was time for her to come home. I went up on Friday morning to help her pack."

"Your timing couldn't have been better," I said. "The Fausts figured out where Mom was and they're probably on their way up there now."

"Boy, are they going to be pissed when they get there and discover she's gone," Kieran remarked with a smirk on his face.

"Yes. They will be angry. And they will come after us. We have to be diligent." Mimi's eyes snapped.

I had a spark of an idea, and I grinned. "I say we beat them at their own game."

"What does that mean, exactly?" Kieran sounded like Hendricks had earlier.

I glanced at Mimi, and then at my mother. "The reason Edison Faust is so motivated to find you, Mom, is that he has a plan." I told my family the story of Jack Hughes' gold. Mimi smiled and nodded as I spoke, understanding immediately what I was thinking. One by one, the rest of my family's faces lit up as they caught on to my idea.

"All we have to do is find the gold before they do," I finished.

"And then we take them down," Kieran added.

"How – how do you know all this about Edison's plan, Raegan?" my dad asked, bewildered.

I took a deep breath and glanced at Mimi and Kieran, who nodded encouragingly.

"Please be kind," I said. And I told my parents everything.

THE END

ACKNOWLEDGMENTS

My undying gratitude goes out to all of my family, friends and colleagues who have offered kind and supportive words throughout my journey. And to my readers, without whom none of this would be possible.

Thank you.

ABOUT THE AUTHOR

Brenda Lyne is the pseudonym of author Jennifer DeVries. Jennifer lives just outside Minneapolis, Minnesota with her two busy kids, two cats, two fish, and probably a partridge in a pear tree. She is living, breathing proof that it is never too late to follow your dreams. *Angel Baby* is her fourth novel.

ALSO AVAILABLE FROM BRENDA LYNE:

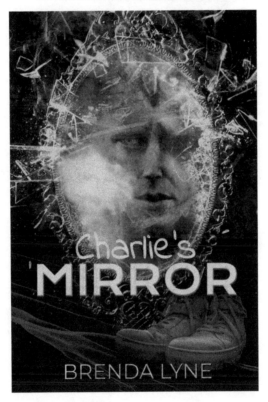

ALSO AVAILABLE FROM BRENDA LYNE:

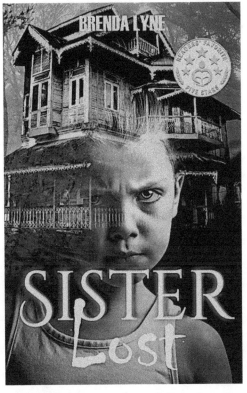

As soon as Lexie Novak and her four-year-old daughter Ava move into the house on Washburn Avenue, the nightmares and strange phenomena begin.

Can Lexie uncover the secrets of the house on Washburn Avenue – and reunite a dying man with his long-lost twin sister – before she becomes the house's next victim?

Available online at brendalyne.com, Amazon, and Barnes & Noble.

ALSO AVAILABLE FROM BRENDA LYNE:

Raegan O'Rourke is a talented investigative reporter with a secret gift: she can touch things and see visions of past events.

Can Raegan use her ability to two lost teenagers home – and live to tell about it?

Available online at brendalyne.com, Amazon, and Barnes & Noble.

Printed in the USA
CPSIA information can be obtained
at www.ICGtesting.com
JSHW010310010823
45654JS00007B/16